Silver World

Also by Cliff McNish

THE SILVER SEQUENCE

The Silver Child
Silver City

THE DOOMSPELL TRILOGY

The Doomspell
The Scent of Magic
The Wizard's Promise

SILVER WORLD

CLIFF McNISH

Orion
Children's Books

First published in Great Britain in 2005
by Orion Children's Books
a division of the Orion Publishing Group Ltd
Orion House
5 Upper St Martin's Lane
London WC2H 9EA

1 3 5 7 9 10 8 6 4 2

A catalogue record for this book is available
from the British Library

Printed in Great Britain by Clays Ltd, St Ives plc

ISBN 1 84255 261 9

www.orionbooks.co.uk

For my brothers – Andy, Paul, Aldous and Mike –
and my sister, Caron.

Contents

1 the barrier   1

2 the loved ones   10

3 a child lit from within   17

4 not in the least human   25

5 need   32

6 starscape   45

7 weapons   54

8 sifts   61

9 drills   71

10 emergence   80

11 a child to catch a child   96

12 bait   105

13 humiliation   118

14 bulk   123

15 the hazel-eyed girl   138

16 carnac   146

17 milo   155

18 the forest of blades   168

19 the blossoming mist   172

20 into the ocean   174

21 a rich and terrifying beauty   178

22 more than human   185

One

the barrier

THOMAS

'He'll never make it,' I said.

It was the usual scene at the Coldharbour Barrier: crowds of young children, all hoping for a glimpse of their parents. Most didn't stand a chance, of course – only the strongest adults were able to force their way to the front of the Barrier.

'There are too many,' I warned Helen. 'If he tries to get any closer he'll be crushed.'

'No, he's nearly pushed his way through.'

'Where?'

'Over there, Thomas.'

I saw him at last – a big man making his way to the Barrier edge.

The last few steps were the most dangerous. Thousands of other parents were jostling for position. If he slipped he'd probably be trampled to death. With great care, making sure not to shove anyone else down into Coldharbour's well-trodden mud, he squeezed past two burly men and one frantic-looking mother.

Helen walked up as close to him as she could. She wasn't crying, though she had been on the way here. As soon as he saw her, she manufactured a smile from somewhere and reached out her hands. At the same time, he pressed his palms against the Barrier. For a moment their fingers were so close that they were almost touching.

'Dad ...' she whispered.

'I know,' he said.

Helen's father. Until this morning, he'd been the only adult inside Coldharbour. He'd been snatched away just after dawn. While he was gathering food at one of the drop-off points, the nearby Barrier edge had simply – moved.

Only a little. Just enough to place his feet outside.

No touching was possible between them now. No talking, either. The invisible boundary that kept adults out of Coldharbour and children inside, once we arrived, didn't allow any communication. All along the Barrier, separated families could only strive to read each others' lips.

Helen, of course, being a mind-reader, was able to do far more than that.

I stayed back to give her a little privacy. She didn't get much time with her dad, though. He was a powerfully built man, and held his ground for longer than most, but he wasn't the only desperate parent, and was soon dragged out of sight.

Helen remained at the Barrier edge for a while, composing herself before she returned to me.

It was hard to believe that only a few weeks had passed since all the children in the world started making their way towards Coldharbour. It wasn't much of a place to come to – just a few miles of nondescript mud bordering the sea.

That hadn't stopped us running crazily towards it, of course. First me, jogging through the night, swinging my plastic carrier bag. Followed by five other special children. Then, once we were there, the others – every single child in the world.

Millions had already squashed themselves inside Coldharbour or spilled out into the surrounding countryside. Those from remoter places were still on their way. Only Helen knew how terrible some of their journeys had become.

'It's not so bad once they can see Milo,' she said, reading my concerns. 'They feel safer then, at least.'

I glanced up, and there he was, the reason we were all huddled in this desolate place: Milo – the silver child. Amazingly, I'd grown used to his gigantic body hovering over us, sometimes close to the ground, sometimes higher, but never straying from Coldharbour's skies. His colossal bald head gleamed like a disc of silvered light. His body was over four miles long. His wings, several times that size, extended so far into the distance that on overcast days you had no idea where the tips ended.

We no longer questioned why Milo was positioned over us. We knew the reason. He was a defender. He was a guardian. He was our shield against a creature approaching the Earth, a creature intent on killing us all. We had no meaningful name for that creature, so we simply called it the Roar. It seemed as good a name as any. After all, almost the only thing we knew about it came from the interminable screams that tore from its lungs night and day.

I say it, but of course I mean *she*. The Roar was female. Helen, slipping into her mind, had discovered that. And the Roar was not alone. Two offspring, her newborn, nestled in the Roar's flesh as she made her way towards the Earth. 'They can't wait to begin feeding on us,' Helen had told me.

'The Roar likes reminding me of that. She does so whenever she can.'

The only information the rest of us had about the Roar came from her screams. They came every few minutes, and each of them started the same way – a low rumble just below the threshold of sound.

One was heading towards Coldharbour now, as Helen and I walked away from the Barrier. This particular scream began in the west, the usual pre-frightener before the full volume arrived. 'Here it comes,' a girl behind us whispered, and everyone in the area tensed, bracing themselves, the smallest children running in all directions, jamming their hands over their ears. They always did that, but it made no difference. The sound couldn't be shut out. Screaming back made no difference, either, though some always tried that as well. This scream was one of the loudest yet, the pitch rising until even the oldest teenagers were gritting their teeth as the full force detonated across Coldharbour.

The reverberations gradually subsided, but nobody relaxed, not yet. The Roar's screams weren't like a single peak of noise. We were never quite certain they were gone. Long afterwards, as if the Roar wanted to keep us on edge, a series of separate concussive shrieks would split across various parts of Coldharbour. The after-screams we called them.

Oh yes. The Roar liked to make us jump.

Helen kept her head down, marching grimly in the direction of our shack.

'How long?' I asked.

'Before the Roar gets here?' She smiled thinly. 'The Roar's not telling me, Thomas. She's keeping that little surprise all to herself. She wants to catch us off guard, especially Milo. The only way we'll get any advance warning is if I can trick it out of her.'

'Can you?'

'No. Not yet, anyway. I might never be able to.' She flicked her shoulder-length brown hair behind her ears. 'You know, I think I understand why Dad was taken now. It's obvious, really.'

'Oh?'

'He wasn't touching the Barrier this morning. He wasn't even that close. He's always been careful about that. It was the Roar. I've been inside her mind so many times that she knows all about me now. She knows how much I've relied on Dad. She moved the Barrier deliberately.'

'Why?'

'To take him away.'

'To isolate you?'

'Yes. To make it harder.'

We made our way further inside Coldharbour. It was a dull morning, with a typically strong wind whipping in off the sea. What I hated about the Coldharbour wind was the way it plucked every whiff from the millions of unwashed children and presented them to my nose.

Not that I smelled any better than the others. Worse probably, since I'd been here the longest.

When I'd first arrived in Coldharbour you could run for miles without seeing anyone. Now you couldn't wriggle your toes without tripping over some little kid or other's outstretched feet. The majority just sat around in the muck, keeping a close eye on Milo and eating a little food whenever any trickled in from the drop-offs. There wasn't much else to do except try to snatch a few winks of sleep between the screams.

Oh, and wait, of course. Wait for the Roar to arrive.

I didn't want to just wait. I wanted to do much more than

that. I had a gift, after all, a gift the twins had called my *beauty*. It was a talent – a power – to reach out to other children and change them. It had helped create Milo, our first defender, and it had also played a part in bringing his five-year-old sister, Jenny, to us. Her body, lit by my beauty, now glowed, attracting the world's animals towards Coldharbour. It was incredible watching them all arrive, but even if every animal somehow became part of our defence I knew we needed more than that. We needed additional child defenders. Where were they? I'd searched endlessly in Coldharbour, hoping to discover them, but if there was a remarkable boy or girl out there waiting for my beauty I hadn't located them yet.

'Maybe they're still on their way by boat,' Helen said. 'Some won't reach us for weeks yet.'

I considered that. If the Roar was close, it meant my beauty might never find the child in time. And even if someone special was already inside Coldharbour, how was I supposed to find one child with all these others in the way? For days I'd felt increasingly frustrated. I'd even started stomping randomly around Coldharbour, hoping my beauty would offer me one of its familiar twitches of interest. Not a murmur, though. Not a tickle of curiosity about anyone. In the battle to come, I'd never felt less certain I could make a difference.

'You need to kick-start that beauty of yours,' Helen said, stepping over a titchy kid. 'I know exactly who you need.'

'Who?'

'The twins.'

I nodded. The twins – Emily and Freda – were two sisters I'd met on a rubbish tip when I first arrived in Coldharbour. That early sight of them skittering about in their weird insect-like way across the garbage had scared me half to death, but it shouldn't have. They knew, you see. They recognized my beauty straightaway; even before I did, they understood what it was for. If there was someone out there thirsting for my beauty, I was sure Emily and Freda would find them.

The twins weren't likely to be back soon, though. For two days, altered by Jenny, they'd been swimming deep inside the Pacific ocean with thousands of other children. They were after something alive on the ocean floor. The Protector, the twins called it: an enemy of the Roar, a huge creature Helen sensed had fought the Roar in the past. Just the idea of the Protector gave us hope, but not much because Helen thought it was imprisoned down there. Shackled somehow, held down.

Even Helen understood almost nothing about the Protector, but the mysterious look she gave me as it came into my mind made me stop.

'You know something new?' I asked.

'Maybe.'

'What?'

'Just a feeling. Nothing really.'

'Come on. You obviously know more than that.'

'It's the twins,' she said. 'They reached the Protector a few hours ago. They're with it now. They're working on the bonds holding its limbs down.' Her eyes shone. 'I think they're on one of the Protector's hands. Its *hands*, Thomas. Over five hundred of the ocean-children are beside them, all working on a single finger, or something like a finger.'

I stared out in the direction of the sea. I didn't like to think of Emily staying down there too long. Twice before in attempting to reach the Protector she'd almost drowned. Only Freda had saved her.

'She's in trouble this time as well,' Helen said.

'What?'

'It's her lungs again.'

'How bad is she?'

'Holding up, no more than that.'

'Why doesn't Freda bring her back, then?' I snapped. 'If –'

'Because Freda doesn't know, that's why. Emily's hiding her pain. Not all of it – Freda's too clever for that – but most of it.'

'I don't understand.'

'Emily doesn't want to leave the Protector, Thomas. The Protector's not something you leave easily, once you've found it. Now she's there, she doesn't ever want to leave it again.'

I thought about that as we trudged across northern Coldharbour. There was no straight path back to our shack. We had to keep detouring around the bigger child-families – groups of mostly smaller kids led by a few older teenagers – and every step of the way Coldharbour's never-ending sea-breeze carried plastic, paper bags, wrappers and other gunk like a whirling tide past our heels.

Sometimes the lighter bits of rubbish rose on updrafts of Milo's wings, too, disturbing the birds.

'There are more today,' I noted.

Helen nodded. 'Jenny's brought in most of them now. All the strongest fliers, anyway.'

I watched as one huge mixed flock, about a mile wide, made a slow curve around Milo's head. Other birds soared across the length of his body, or lodged themselves in the crevasses of his wings. They were a bizarre enough sight, but it was the insect swarms that really freaked me out. Dense patches of them rested all over Milo. They were everywhere: in the folds of his neck, along the miles of his shoulders, even nestling in the silver hollows of his ears. For the past two days they'd been steadily flying in. And big land mammals were making their ways towards us, too. I'd lost count of the number I'd seen lumbering up to the Barrier edge, scaring the life out of the parents. Even Coldharbour's grey, scummy estuary was full of new arrivals. Fish mostly, though I'd heard reports about sharks.

'All the animals will make it here eventually,' Helen said. 'If they can. If the journey's not too far. It's their Earth as well, after all. They'll make the same stand we do against the Roar.'

I had my doubts about that. Milo was one thing, but what difference could even large animal predators make against a creature the size of the Roar?

'Teeth and jaws,' Helen said. 'They'll be just as determined as us. And don't forget: most animals spend their lives fighting to eat or stay alive. They're good at it.' She smiled slightly. 'They're better at it than us.'

'I still can't see a shoal of sharks hurting the Roar.'

'On its own, a single shoal, you'd be right,' Helen answered. 'But imagine Milo attacking the Roar, then add all the animals, all the creatures in the ocean and anything that can fly. Imagine, when the Roar launches her strike, every insect and every bird seeking out her eyes.'

Two

the loved ones

HELEN

Thomas wasn't convinced by my argument about the sharks, but as we tramped back to the shack I wasn't thinking about that. I could only think about one thing: Dad.

He was gone. How could he be gone? During my visit to the Barrier, I'd rehearsed the words I'd mouth to him, but I should have known I'd fall to pieces when we were face-to-face. I hadn't been able to think of a single thing to say. For most of the time we'd just stared at one another, with Dad attempting to control his emotions and silently express his trust in me.

I was grateful for Thomas's company on that visit, but afterwards all I really wanted to do was shut out all the yammering minds of Coldharbour. So, while Thomas went off on one of his beauty-hunts, I squatted down on my jacket and tried to relax in the sun.

The sky. The weather. No feelings to bother me there, at least. Only Milo's head, hanging like a great moon between the clouds. As I peered up at him, his face seemed so serene and untroubled. He had a way of staring out implacably over the sea as if nothing ever disturbed him. If you watched for long enough, you could easily believe he might single-handedly fight off the Roar. Even the adults crammed against the Barrier had started to believe it. Gazing up at Milo they didn't see a child. They saw something more; something greater.

I didn't blame them for that, but beneath all that verve of wing I knew Milo was far from untroubled. I'd realized for some time that the Protector was in his mind, preparing him for the Roar's challenge, but there wasn't enough time for Milo to learn every defence. The Roar was an experienced murderer. Her mind was too powerful for me to shut out altogether, and to frighten me she'd reminded me several times how expert a killer she was: how skilled, how proven an assassin, how long she had spent perfecting all the ways to overcome a Protector's defences.

And Milo, I knew, no matter how well he fought, did not have the strength of a Protector.

Perversely, this morning, as soon as I discovered Dad was outside the Barrier, I'd sent my mind out to the Roar. Usually Dad was always with me when I did that, but I knew I shouldn't wait – that if I didn't go immediately to locate the Roar without him beside me, later the courage would be harder to find.

And this is what had happened: the Roar, for once, hadn't guarded her mind from me. On the contrary, she was almost gracious. She'd lowered her defences. She and her newborn invited me in.

A sort of welcome.

And what an idiot I'd been, just stepping into her trap. I did pull away, but not before I'd felt her mind roving over my body, as if testing each link in my spine. 'When I arrive, I won't kill you myself,' she'd told me. 'The newborn will do it. That is the only encouragement they need to complete the last of the journey.' She'd thanked me for that, and then added, 'We have a name for your friends, Helen. Thomas, Walter, Jenny, and the twins – the loved ones. You should have hidden them from me. The newborn will kill each one individually, *before* they kill you.'

A sudden commotion brought my attention back to Coldharbour. It was a large mixed pod of dolphins, arriving just off the south-western shore.

'Where? Where are they?' a small boy near me called out, wanting to see them. An older girl hoisted him onto her shoulders.

'Higher!' the boy cried, still not able to see.

All across Coldharbour it was happening, the leaders of the child-families raising the smallest boys and girls up to look at the ocean. I looked with them, and felt a sudden stab of joy as I stole into the youngsters' excited minds. Part of me wanted to stay with them as long as I could. Instead, my thoughts strayed elsewhere – to a group in trouble under Coldharbour.

The Unearthers.

One reason Thomas was so concerned about finding the right child for his beauty was that he'd previously given some of it to the wrong children. He'd found them scraping rocks against their faces, and his beauty replaced their hands with drills. Thomas thought they were drilling for something to help Milo. He was wrong. The Unearthers were trying to dig Carnac from the core of the world. We all knew that name

now: Carnac, largest offspring of the Roar, left by her on our
world ages ago to mature and finally take his pick of the food
running around. Us.

Carnac had taken control of the Unearthers' minds, and
by the time Jenny released them they were ugly to behold –
metal-bodied, with massive shoulders to take the impact of
the drills. I'd seen some courageous acts since I arrived in
Coldharbour, but I think the bravest was what the
Unearthers did after Jenny freed them. They didn't cringe
under Milo's wings, bemoaning the loss of their hands. No.
They went back into their drill-holes. They went back down
underground. To wait for Carnac. To fight him if they could.

Their task was harder than ours. On the surface, at least
we had Milo. Under Coldharbour, there was only the rough
feel of the rocks to guide them.

Their leader, Tanni, and his drill-partner, Parminder, were
currently crouched in a tight tunnel over four miles below
us. For several hours the temperature had been steadily rising inside the steel of their bodies.

'It's too dark,' Parminder was whispering. 'Just too dark
for us. We'll never see Carnac approach. Not well enough to
be able to fight him properly.'

'We'll hear him no matter what,' Tanni replied. 'There'll
be some part of him we can fix onto. There's bound to be.'

'Let's go higher,' Parminder suggested. 'We're at our limit
at this depth. There's not enough air.'

'I know, but if there's a chance of staying here I'd like to.
I want to attack Carnac as soon as he makes his move. That
way, as he pushes through to the surface, we'll have more
time to use the drills.'

'How do you know the drills will stop him?'

Tanni didn't answer that. He had no idea whether or not
the drills would even slow up Carnac. He hoped they would,

that's all. He sat hunched in the suffocating dark with the other Unearthers, waiting to find out.

I left them, drew back, and made my usual quick scan across Coldharbour. Dad was safe. So was Thomas. Walter was watching over Jenny. For a while I spread my thoughts in a wider compass, taking in as many of those children still trying to reach Coldharbour as I could. I'm not sure what I expected to find. Maybe the first signs of the defender Thomas kept hoping so desperately for. But if anyone extraordinary was out there I couldn't detect them. Finally I sent my mind to the place I always went in search of a little hope.

The twins.

Emily and Freda were seven miles under the Pacific. Nestled against one of the Protector's vast hand-like appendages, they were rubbing their nails raw along the edge of something like a pale finger. It stretched down and away from them into the rock. Other children were lying against the Protector's lips, or climbing over its neck, or the bruised areas surrounding its single eye. A ruined eye. I sensed that. Whatever was down there was virtually blind.

Ill as it was, the Protector's huge body gave off a dazzling silver brightness. Emily's face, lit by it, was blanched white. Her red hair streamed on a cold gentle current towards Freda. They gazed intently at each other. All around them hundreds of children, numb-fingered, their lips frozen, scratched away, working to free the same part of the Protector's hand. As Emily straightened her back and yanked, a link of flesh momentarily unclenched.

I felt a sigh from the Protector. The feeling of movement again.

'If I'd more of its hand,' Emily mouthed at Freda, 'I'd stroke it.'

'If I'd more of its hand,' Freda mouthed back, 'I'd sway inside it.'

They blinked slowly at one another.

'You don't look well, Emms,' Freda said. 'Are your lungs complaining at you? What yer hiding from me?'

'Nothin',' Emily answered, turning away. 'We ain't gonna fail, Free. Not this time. We come this far. We won't fail now, will we?'

I wanted to stay with them, but my thoughts were snapped back to Coldharbour.

It was the Roar, choosing this moment to remind us of her presence.

It hadn't been long since the last of her screams. This one broke more piercingly than usual across Coldharbour, sending the smallest children scrambling for cover. A few teenagers swore defiantly at the sky. The rest gazed up at Milo. Who stayed entirely still. Who did not move at all. Deliberately. Milo made a point of never showing any anxiety when one of the Roar's screams splintered over us. He always remained impassive, knowing how frightened people would be if he gave any other reaction.

OK, I thought. All right, Helen. Stop putting it off. You know what you have to do.

I finished picking my way across northern Coldharbour. When I reached the shack I shut the door firmly behind me. Then I barred the door using Thomas's bed. I needed complete privacy for what I was about to attempt.

A visit of the mind. A visit to the Roar.

I didn't want to go back to her so soon after the fiasco this morning, but I knew I had to. Recently the Roar's screams had become louder and more frequent. Why? Just to frighten us? Or because she was closer?

Only one way to find out.

'Come on,' I thought. 'Don't blunder in. For once, try not to let her know you're on your way. Gently. Surprise her.'

I lay back on my mattress. I'd never found a way to ease the feeling of dread before a visit to the Roar, and this time was no different. I kicked off my shoes and rubbed my toes. When that didn't make me feel any better, I eavesdropped on the thoughts of a few of the more confident minds in Coldharbour, hoping their self-assurance would rub off on me. It didn't. Finally, I joined both hands lightly over my stomach. For a moment I pretended that Dad was next to me.

No more delays. Blinking twice, I pushed my mind out into space.

Three

a child lit from within

THOMAS

After another pointless beauty-wander, around southern Coldharbour this time, I made my way northwards again between the child-families. A young boy bumped into me at one point. He glanced up sharply, then turned away again.

My beauty didn't stir. Wishful thinking, I thought.

As I neared the shack, there was one area not crammed with children. It was a clearing – a place you could stretch out.

A girl lingered in that clearing. A little five-year-old girl. Her legs were planted firmly in Coldharbour's mud. Her arms were open as if waiting for something. Her longish light-brown hair billowed this way and that in the breeze.

Jenny.

From a distance she looked more like a statuette of a

child lit from within than a real girl. She shone. Her entire body gleamed. She stood in exactly the same spot she had done for days, simply glowing. Her skin was almost translucent. Light burst in layers from her face. It was a light to entice the world's animals towards Coldharbour, and Jenny would have been surrounded by them were it not for Walter.

He stayed at permanent attention near her, all twelve-foot giant of him, keeping them away.

It was the twins who'd first led me to Walter. We'd found him stirring the embers of a fire with his oversized hands, and he'd terrified me, too – until I saw that great lopsided grin of his.

Right now, Jenny had all his attention. The larger animals weren't the problem – they mostly stayed at Coldharbour's perimeter, rubbing shoulders uneasily with the parents. It was the insects. They were naturally drawn to light and nothing, of course, had ever glowed quite like Jenny.

Since even Walter's enormous arms could only swish at the flies, he'd established better defences – the bonfires. They burned all around Jenny, tended night and day by the small kids who followed Walter everywhere, the ones he called his 'visitors'. I'd lost count of how many visitors Walter had, but he'd certainly put them to good use lately, either feeding the fires or gathering up rubbish to fuel them. When someone told Walter that insects couldn't stand the scent of citronella plants, he'd put in an order for them at the drop-offs. He got them, too.

Our Walter could be persuasive when he wanted to be.

He stood near Jenny at all times. 'Keeping her company,' as he put it. I say near, because the light radiating from Jenny had a burning quality, and only Walter could stand being within touching distance. He sometimes got himself in trouble too, because instead of just handing Jenny a bit of food and drink he usually stayed long enough 'to have a bit of a talk'. Plenty of times I'd seen him chatting casually away with her as if he had all day to spend, his neck slowly roasting. Helen and I tried to stop him, but it was hard to make Walter do anything he didn't want to.

As I approached the clearing he spotted me and lumbered over, offering one of his wide disarming grins.

'All r-right, Tommy?'

'Yep,' I said. 'You?'

'Good. R-real good.' He indicated with satisfaction the tremendous amount of rubbish his visitors had managed to collect. Enough to keep the fires going for at least five years. While we chatted a bird swooped down, attempting a kamikaze landing on Jenny. You should have seen Walter move to stop it. The bird didn't even get close.

'Looks like your skin's about to peel off, Walter,' I told him, when he came back.

'I'm all right,' he said defensively, dabbing at his smoky red face. 'G-got a towel now. Don't get so b-burned as I did.'

He was limping. It wasn't an injury. It was the home-made shoes Emily and Freda had given him as a birthday present before they left for the ocean. One of the shoes was barely hanging on, but Walter kept wearing it out of sheer stubbornness. He'd developed a way of shuffling his right foot to keep it on.

'Must be tricky,' I said. 'When you have to run, I mean.'

'It's f-fine,' he said, shoving in his toes.

Everyone in Coldharbour was shabby these days, but Walter outdid us all. After his battle with the Unearthers, his clothes looked like they'd been through several good shredders. I couldn't help thinking of the twins. If they'd still been with us, his jacket would have been patched up long ago. Not that Walter cared what he looked like. He was more interested in keeping Jenny free from insects.

'Smoke's w-working,' he said, happily watching the grey coils snake up from the fires.

'Yeah, right,' I said. 'Kids are choking, and for about a mile around no one can see anything, but I suppose that's OK.'

Walter stiffened, gazed around, saw that I was exaggerating, and grinned. 'Just have to acc-acc–' He started again. 'Just have to acc–' His stutter didn't like that word. With dignity, he said, 'They'll just have to p-put up with it. Jenny n-needs the smoke. Midges, they d-don't like the smoke, Toms.'

'They don't like you, either.'

He grunted, shuffling across to a couple of youngsters who weren't fanning the smoke the proper way.

It had taken Walter ages to get the fires positioned perfectly. Too close and the smoke went in Jenny's eyes. Too far away and the flies took their chances. A tricky balance. Walter had his visitors working at it twenty-four hours a day. I'd never heard a single one of them complain.

Many of the visitors had willingly become sentries, too, keeping an eye out for danger. Walter helped them construct steel and concrete look-out towers throughout Coldharbour, from which they periodically sent signals back. A single raised arm meant all was OK. The closest tower was about half a mile from the shack. The three small children manning it looked horribly exposed.

'When she attacks, the Roar's bound to see the towers first,' I'd told him, wondering if he'd thought it through.

'That's right,' Walter replied.

'What? Are you saying you want to put the tower kids in danger?'

'No.' When I still didn't understand, he spelt it out. 'The Roar isn't interested in the v-visitors, except as food. She'll come after you f-first, Tommy, if she can. You, Jenny and Helen. I d-don't want that to happen.'

I hadn't thought of that – the towers as a distraction. It gave them a chilling new perspective.

Walter had other defences as well – tunnels throughout Coldharbour. They wouldn't be much use if Carnac came up right under us, but Walter reckoned that if the Roar attacked from the sky we'd be harder to locate underground. He made me and Helen practise, too, timing how fast we scuttled down whatever tunnel was closest. Sometimes we went in the tunnel with Walter, sometimes without him.

'Just in c-case,' he explained. In case, of course, for whatever reason, he wasn't there when the Roar attacked. I didn't like to think about that.

Walter, still smarting over the way the Unearthers had surprised him when they surrounded the shack, encouraged his visitors to sneak up on him. They did their best, and were inventive enough, but never once caught him off guard. It's pretty hard to sneak up on someone who never sleeps. Walter never even rested, not really. Once I thought I'd caught him napping, but then the lid of one of his big eyes opened as I tiptoed past his chest. Nights were when he was most alert. 'The Roar's in s-space,' he'd explained. 'She must be used to the dark. Children d-don't like darkness, Tommy. I'd attack then. Wouldn't y-you?'

From my position now, a stone's throw from the fires, I could hear Jenny's high-pitched, lilting voice.

'She's singing,' Walter said, surprised that I didn't understand.

'Singing?'

'Rhymes the t-twins taught her before they went away. Means she's s-scared, Tommy. Jenny g-gets that way sometimes. Lonely, you know. She sings when she g-gets that way. Excuse me.'

Walter's visitors anxiously wrapped a wet blanket over his head and shoulders, and he rushed off. I had to squint to follow him.

When he reached Jenny she pushed him away.

'Go back!' she demanded. 'Go back or you'll be hurt! I've told you, Walter! I've told you!'

'B-but you're singing.'

'I know. Go away!'

'Let me c-cover you up. Just your f-face, that's all. Let me –'

'No!'

Jenny never let him wrap anything over her skin. She needed it exposed to attract the animals. She put up with the few flies that got through the smoke. On this occasion, though, as Walter ran across and offered her a sip of water, I noticed that she was smiling.

'It's all right,' she said, levering herself up on his arm. 'It's better now. They're coming. They're coming to protect us. They're here.'

I had no idea what Jenny meant, but from one of the visitor towers came a cross-handed signal only Walter could interpret.

'Hey!' I shouted.

I must have sounded nervous, because Walter sprang across and automatically checked me over for possible injuries.

'I'm OK,' I said. 'But what's going on?'

A hush had descended over Coldharbour's shore.

Gradually that hush made its way towards us in the north as children turned towards the ocean. Soon even parents at the Barrier were straining to see. When they couldn't, they did what everyone else did – instinctively looked up at Milo for reassurance.

And Milo moved; not much; a single wing beat, as if to steady himself.

'What's happening, Walter?'

He reached down and lifted me onto his neck. From there I could see beyond the child-families to the distant waves. And what I saw was this: new animals arriving along Coldharbour's shore.

I'd already seen gatherings of big mammals at the boundaries of Coldharbour, but this was different. From wherever they once lived, the biggest of all had come. Perhaps, being so intelligent, they'd decided to travel in strength of numbers, and met in mid-ocean before setting off for Coldharbour. Whatever the reason, all the shoals arrived at once. Who knows how far some of them had journeyed, but it was a sight to behold, all those dark backs breaking the surface waters at the same time. I glanced at Jenny, and there was an expression of joy on her face I'd only ever seen that first day she wandered into Coldharbour and discovered Walter.

For one extraordinary moment I thought our guests were going to come ashore. I thought they were about to beach themselves and wriggle their broad bellies up onto the sand towards Jenny. They didn't do that, of course. These animals weren't simple flies, knowing no better than to follow a brighter light than the sun. They organized themselves. They took their time, each species making sure their families were together. Only then did we see their great heads rear up from the waters.

'They're m-making a shape,' Walter murmured.

It was a line, a long, tight defensive formation close to the shore. Then, as if practising for what was to come, all the whales turned outward, their mouths open.

Four

not in the least human

HELEN

I'd visited the mind of the Roar several times before. On every one of those visits it had taken me some time to find her; there had always been long stretches of stars between us.

Not this time. Almost immediately – there she was. That was the shock: finding her so fast.

She was far closer than she'd led me to believe on my last visit.

No distance at all.

She'd speeded up. To catch us off guard, I realized.

I found her so rapidly that for once the Roar was not quite prepared for my intrusion. She reacted fast enough once she knew, though: twisting her body, rotating at tremendous speed. Why? Meanwhile, her two newborn attempted to empty their minds. It was a trick the Roar had taught them in response to my probes. One did so successfully. The second, the newborn that had made mistakes before, could not contain its sense of anticipation that the journey was nearly over, and let slip a detail – the sun.

They could see our sun now. That's how close they were.

I gasped, pulled away – and, under me, felt a lurch.

Another mind.

Somehow I knew at once it was the Protector.

It, too, clearly sensed the nearness of the Roar.

I felt a huge convulsion in the Pacific then, a moment of sheer panic from it. Emily, Freda and the rest of the ocean-children were swept away from the Protector's body, across the dark current. But the twins led them back, and soon all of the children were clawing again at the finger.

'We'll work more,' Emily thought, rubbing away at the Protector's encrusted skin. 'We'll work harder. What do you need? We'll stay with you.'

And then I sensed this: the Protector, knowing it had frightened the ocean-children, sending through to them waves of apology and reassurance. Followed by this:

'At last, through this turmoil of ages, I have reached you.'

Those were the first words I heard from the Protector.

They came from the heart of the ocean, oddly light, vaguely female yet not in the least human. And behind the words was a hint of mortality, of nearness to death. In that single instant of contact I realized that the Protector was a virtually immortal being, and that to such a being the prospect of losing its life was more terrifying than any of us could comprehend. Then the Protector closed off that thought as unworthy of its first contact with me, and I was addressed by name.

'Finally, Helen, you can hear me.'

Not a she, I thought. He. Somehow the Protector sounded more male than female.

A laugh greeted that, that I needed to decide male from female.

'Then male I shall be,' the Protector said. 'To the Roar I am no more or less.'

I thought, '*What ... are you?*'

'A guardian. Your world's guardian. I have always been, and only death will make it otherwise.'

I waited, unsure what to ask next.

'Various thoughts I have also kept to myself,' the Protector said. 'One is that Emily will not survive if she stays, and she will stay too long unless pushed away. What would you do, Helen?'

The Protector let me think about that. I realized he was trying to teach me something.

'If it came to it, I would not permit her to die,' the Protector said, 'yet sometimes the mind must learn to control the anxiety it feels for those it loves, Helen. Freda will know when she needs to draw her sister away. As she knew before, so she does now.'

There was a pause. Then the Protector went on, 'I have not told those with me how near the Roar is, for why should I burden them with that? Why humble them before her? Why frighten them more?' Another pause. 'You wondered why our enemy rotated, when you sought her out. It was to prevent you fixing her position and distance using the stars. The Roar forgets you do not have such skill, though I have.' Then the Protector's mind moved amongst the ocean-children, naming them individually for me. 'Have more faith,' he said, when he reached the end. 'They are stronger than they think; and so are you and, perhaps, so am I.'

His voice trembled, and I realized it was pain that made it do so.

Again that expansive laughter. 'Pain is endurable, Helen, though I would wish to have endured less. I have a request. Keep Jenny close. With the help of the ocean-children I may break these bonds, but whether I do or not Jenny is still the key.'

'I know,' I said. 'The animals ...'

'Yes, but there is a still greater purpose she offers. Only you can provide – wait! You have not silenced your mind!'

I jumped. It was true. I had been so astonished to hear the Protector's thoughts that I'd forgotten to guard my own from the Roar for the last few moments. I experienced a pang of unbearable loss as the Protector drew back from me.

Followed by a surge of confidence.

The Roar had been listening in. If she'd been in any doubt before about the pitiful state of the Protector, now she knew for certain. I sensed the second newborn turn its blunt head with satisfaction towards its mother, then. Despite its many blunders on the voyage, it knew it had not made a mistake as important as this.

For the remainder of the day I nursed my guilt. How could I have been so careless, so stupid? The Protector didn't contact me again, though I was desperate for him to. I would have tried to find him if I'd not suspected that the Roar and her newborn were eavesdropping.

Then, in the evening, with Thomas off on another wander around Coldharbour, this happened: Jenny stopped shining.

She simply stopped.

Pulling on my coat, I hurried from the shack to the bonfires.

On the way, I saw the consequences: insects flying confusedly in many directions, birds rising in their great variegated flocks. From the perimeter of Coldharbour animals every-where were on the move.

'Walter ...'

Jenny stood blinking at him, in the clearing between the fires.

All her light had faded. She was just herself again. She looked lost and small beside him.

'I'm dirty,' she said wretchedly. 'Help me. I've been a good girl, haven't I?'

Now that she was no longer shining, Jenny's face could be seen properly for the first time in two days. It was virtually black from all the smoke. Her hair was matted with sweat, her cheeks flushed with heat. She tottered up to lean against Walter's legs, gathering the filthy dressing gown around her. Wrinkling her nose, she reached up to wipe a sleeve against his chest.

A flock of gulls wheeled overhead, away from Milo's wings. Kittiwakes followed, and doves flew along the coast. Jenny didn't even glance up.

'You've f-forgotten the animals,' Walter told her. 'Don't you know they n-need you?'

She shrugged. 'Flies,' she said, sniffing her hair. 'Sometimes they got on me. I told you, but they still did. I told you.'

'I'm here for you,' Walter said, trying to make her understand. 'Who have these animals g-got except you? If they go too f-far, the Roar will get them.'

'No,' I told him. 'It's OK. It's not what you think.'

The animals weren't leaving, I realized. Jenny just didn't need to glow any more to keep them inside Coldharbour. Something new was developing between her and them. Even Jenny didn't understand it yet.

She blinked, playing with a tear in Walter's jacket.

He carried her inside his own hut and helped her wash. The twins had taught Jenny a level of cleanliness she'd never worried about before coming to Coldharbour, and she took her time, insisting her nails were immaculately clean. By the time I went inside, her undergarments and dressing gown had been replaced by a bright red dress – borrowed from one of Walter's visitors.

Jenny twirled in it, then led us outside.

Birds were standing just beyond the threshold of the hut. Hundreds of them.

As soon as Jenny emerged they formed themselves into straight lines – orderly rows, wings neatly folded. Looking into Jenny's mind, I knew she'd organized them this way to impress me and Walter.

'See!' she cried, skipping in a wide circle. 'See!'

'Good. V-very good,' Walter said, glancing uneasily at me. 'What else … can you d-do?'

Jenny playfully lifted her arms and more birds flew down to take their places in the rows.

But not all the birds. The more distant ones paid her no attention at all. And something else: the more she added to her rows the less tidy the rows became. Several birds lost interest altogether and simply flew off. There were obviously limits to her control.

Jenny was upset, but too tired to try to bring the birds back. I wasn't surprised. She'd been standing up for two full days. She needed sleep. I searched her mind for other things to soothe her.

'Give her a doll,' I whispered to Walter. 'She hasn't played with one for ages. Not the old mud dolls of the twins. They're falling to bits. Borrow one off one of your visitors.' He waited for anything else. 'Just comfort her,' I told him. 'Take her to your hut. She's missed you more than anything.

I'll make sure no one disturbs you.'

As early afternoon settled over Coldharbour, Jenny fell asleep in Walter's arms. I thought her control of the birds would disappear when that happened, but I was wrong. They gathered in ever larger numbers around Walter's hut. As the sun dipped under one of Milo's wings, a few dragon-flies alighted in the baked mud. Their rainbow-coloured wings twitched in the breeze as they waited patiently for Jenny to reawaken.

Five

need

THOMAS

As soon as I saw the gulls take flight from Milo's wings, I knew something had happened.

I hurried north again, but I was miles away. For ages I'd been wandering around Coldharbour's eastern mud flats. I'd gone there because I didn't know the area, and hoped to find some child pining for my beauty.

It was ridiculous. Although I hadn't admitted it to anyone else, over the last few hours I'd become so desperate to feel a snatch of beauty inside me again that I'd taken to running around Coldharbour. For a while I convinced myself this was sensible behaviour, that I was just searching for someone who needed my beauty, but I couldn't keep up the pretence for long. The truth was that anyone who so much as turned in my direction had me breathless with anticipation. The smallest glance, and my heart raced.

One girl gave me a smile. I knew she was only being

friendly, but I had to be sure. I think that's when I lost it completely, because I grabbed her. She took one look at the disturbing expression on my face and hurried off.

I didn't blame her. What was going on? Every child in Coldharbour suddenly seemed like an intriguing prospect for my beauty!

Eventually I lost my composure altogether and set about bumping into people, deliberately trying to trigger a response. Anyone who looked or behaved differently interested me. I found myself following a girl with a patch over her left eye. I wanted so badly to take a look under that patch, but resisted the urge. Later I wished I hadn't, and spent half an hour trying to find her again.

I even got myself into a fight with a teenage boy. He wasn't doing anything wrong. He just didn't get out of my way fast enough.

One bruised lip later, a bizarre idea jumped into my head – that maybe the next child who needed my beauty was *stuck* somewhere. That's why they haven't found me, I reasoned. Because they can't! They're not able to walk or something. So I proceeded to check out anyone lying down. It was pathetic. For ages I followed a boy on crutches. Anyone with an awkward walking style attracted my attention. In the slippery mud of Coldharbour there were plenty of those.

Finally one small girl took pity on me. She tried to calm me down and get me to join her child-family. I pulled away lamely – though not before I'd checked them out, made absolutely sure no one in that child-family sharpened the interest of my beauty.

What was wrong with me? What on earth was wrong?

The possibility that there was *no one* out there waiting for my beauty – well, I couldn't bear thinking about that. There had to be. I was so desperate that I stopped feeling embarrassed by my behaviour. I didn't care what people thought any more. I just focused on putting my fingers on as many children as possible. Touching their skin. That was obviously the thing to do. Hadn't my beauty been triggered by the Unearthers when they touched me?

I only stopped when the gulls started wheeling overhead. Jenny.

I knew at once that she was responsible. I knew even before I saw the animals moving along the outskirts of Coldharbour. I set off northwards, following the smoke of Walter's fires.

But on the way I stopped.

Welcome back, I thought, much-missed friend.

My beauty had returned.

At first I expected it to be for one of the children nearest me. I grabbed the closest person – a girl – and introduced myself. Not a flicker of interest.

Then I knew. I suddenly knew exactly who my beauty was intended for, and I ran. Pushing people aside, cursing at them to get out of my way, I made it back to Walter's well-tended fires in less than two hours.

Helen and Walter were waiting for me outside his hut.

'Where is she?' I demanded.

Walter motioned at the door, and Helen said, 'Open it, Walter. Hurry.'

'B-but she's asleep – '

'No, not any more.'

Seeing Helen, I realized that my face must be wild. Walter opened the door, and I didn't wait, I went straight inside.

And there she was, sitting cross-legged on the floor. I could tell at once that Jenny needed to see me as much as I needed to see her. She got up off the floor. She rubbed sleep out of her eyes. She took a step towards me. She was trembling. She looked almost frightened.

Walter was nearby, and I thought Jenny would go straight to him, as she always did when she was scared. But no: she walked hesitantly across the floor of the hut towards me.

And I felt – what? I wasn't sure. Exhilaration. That's what I felt. Sheer heart-thumping exhilaration. Jenny was panting. So was I. We were both breathing at the same accelerated rate – as if our bodies were linked.

My beauty hadn't done anything yet, but I knew it would. Jenny came very close. Was she meant to?

'I don't know,' I said – and for some reason we both laughed.

Inside I felt a tightening, as if atom by atom we were being drawn together. My beauty gathered. It gathered and gathered, yet unbelievably it still did nothing. Was it me who wasn't ready for this yet, or Jenny?

Then she touched me. She didn't lunge out, didn't do it in a hurried way. She touched me – and I couldn't describe everything I felt. It was her eyes. The sockets were still, but the irises moved. They narrowed, then dilated, the irises broad, spread wide, locked into me. Those eyes! I felt suddenly clumsy. I didn't know what I felt.

No one intervened. Walter wanted to join us, but Helen warned him back. I don't know how long Jenny and I stayed like this. We didn't speak. We didn't need words. Her small head was a little on one side. The fingers of both her hands were dug, not harshly, into my head. She pulled it towards her.

Then the Roar screamed, and I think if anything could have broken whatever was silently unfolding between me and Jenny it was that scream. The scream resounded over Coldharbour, the loudest any of us had ever heard. But it made no difference. Not to us. Not to me and Jenny. We barely noticed it.

'Thomas,' she murmured. 'Thomas ...'

She pulled my face down so it touched hers. Her body was still. Her face was still. Her eyes were alive. Then Jenny took my beauty. She tore it out of me the way a famished child might tear fruit from a bush; all at once. It was painful, but I couldn't resist. I didn't want to resist. I looked at her thin strong hands. I followed her beauty-hungry eyes. She drew me closer to her face. The Roar screamed again but it did not matter.

Then a hand dropped on my back. It wasn't Jenny, or Walter, though he was standing close.

Helen.

She was outlined in the hut doorway. A straight spear of Milo's silver light moulded the silhouette of her shoulders against the entrance. I started to speak, but I couldn't. I didn't know what this meant. I didn't know what to say.

'What's ... happening?' I breathed.

'I don't know,' she answered.

I turned back to Jenny. I stared at her, and Jenny stared back, her dilated irises slim and broad, wide and dark.

Then, briefly, her eyes disappeared altogether.

Only the whites were visible, streaked with blue veins at the corners.

Jenny turned away from me. She had the beauty she needed. Suddenly she was only interested in one person.

Her emptied eyes left me and focused on Helen.

'What is it?' I croaked.

'Jenny's expecting something from me,' Helen said.

'Expecting what?'

'I ... don't know.'

Jenny couldn't bear Helen's uncertainty. She left me, ran

across the floor and clutched her waist. 'It's you!' Jenny
shouted at her. 'Don't you know yet? Don't you know,
Helen? It's you! It's only you left now. It's *you* I need.'

'I don't understand,' Helen said. 'I – '

Jenny shook with frustration. 'Don't you know? Don't
you see? You need to find me things! You need to *show* me
things!'

'What things?'

'Things to do! Things to be! Things to *be*!'

With Helen still confused, Jenny howled. It was like an
animal howling, the way she lifted her eyes when she did it.
There was nothing held back. It was so unexpected and so
shocking that I felt the hair rise on my neck. Walter bent
down to her. He picked her up. He stroked her forehead,
drawing two nervous fingers across it.

And that's when Jenny changed.

It didn't happen gradually, but immediately. One moment
Jenny was in Walter's arms, wearing a red dress and reaching
out for Helen. The next we couldn't see her. We could only
see the place where Jenny should have been.

Walter gasped, clutching the space as if he had dropped
her.

'I'm still here,' Jenny squealed. 'Don't let go of me!'

Walter carefully held her up, a space between his hands.

'You c-can still see her,' he murmured.

He was right. If you focused not on where Jenny was but
the background, you could make out her outline. She was
still with us, only –

'Camouflaged,' Helen said. 'Jenny, what are you like this
for?'

'Help me,' Jenny's voice pleaded. 'I can't do it on my own.
I can't!'

Helen walked over to her, found her hands. 'I don't

understand. What do you need from me?'

'Show me what to do!' Jenny shrieked. 'Show me about the Roar! Show me! Show me more about the Roar!'

Still baffled, Helen shook her head, and Jenny tried to explain, but she couldn't and then she gave up trying. In a tired voice she finally said, 'Walter, put me down, please.'

He did, waiting until he heard the tap of her shoes to be sure her feet were on the ground. A moment later Jenny's body made a slight depression on the empty bed. The covers were lifted and we saw the mud dolls of the twins weave in the air as Jenny drew them inside with her. There were a few sniffles, then nothing more. Walter cradled the place where her head was, and soon we heard more regular, deep breaths.

Helen stared at me, trembling slightly. 'I don't know what's happening, Thomas. I've no idea what Jenny expects of me. No idea at all.'

'She's taken a lot of my beauty,' I said. 'I can't believe how much she's taken.'

'She doesn't know why, though. She expects *me* to know, but I don't.'

'What should we do?'

'Let Walter stay with her for now. Jenny's still tired. Let's see what she's like after she's had more sleep. I need ... time to think about this.' She gave me a strange look. 'Anyway, what about you? How do *you* feel?'

I shrugged. I felt a mixture of things. Eager, nervous, scared, uncertain. Then I laughed as I realized what I felt most of all. The words surprised me when they came out, as I had no idea what they meant.

'I feel ready,' I said.

Jenny spent the rest of the day and the first part of the evening alone with Walter in his hut. She didn't wake.

Whenever I visited her, there was nothing new to see – just a blank space on a bed. Later, during the night, Walter came out, seemingly alone, but his hand held something, and I knew it must be Jenny.

I could barely make her out. She sat on top of Walter's raised hand, and through her body I could see the sky. The outline of her head was filled by an edge of Milo's wing.

A wing through her face.

Walter strode over to me and Helen. 'Jenny wants you both to be with her,' he announced. 'She wants you to s-stay with her tonight.'

We didn't question that. Without understanding why, Helen and I both followed Walter into his hut to be close to Jenny, knowing that it felt right. I hauled my own mattress from the shack and spread it out on the floor. Helen curled up beside Walter's feet. Through a crack in the roof, Milo's silver light shone down on us. I sat on the floor near Jenny's bed, not sure how close I should be. Jenny gradually inched nearer to me. I knew because I could feel her shallow breath on my face.

Later she got off the bed and crept down onto the floor, tucking herself up beside me. Her breath was sweet and light. For a while I listened to the sounds of other children around the hut, preparing themselves for the usual restless night interrupted by the Roar. Helen, Jenny and I lay close to one another. We didn't speak but we couldn't sleep either. The night gradually deepened and cooled, and at some point I pulled a blanket around me.

Once he was sure we didn't need him in the hut, Walter squeezed his bulk out of the door and went outside. I heard him telling his visitors that the fires would no longer be needed. Then he arranged the visitors defensively around the hut. I had no idea how many were out there, but there were plenty. Walter kept on the move, as if expecting a surprise attack. There was a rhythm to his tread: stride, stop, pivot – you could almost hear his heavy head turning sharply this way and that – then he'd move on again. He never strayed far from the hut. From time to time he opened the door slightly to check on us.

'He's worried,' Helen told me.

'Of course he is! The things happening to Jenny –'

'No, it's not just Jenny, Thomas. He's worried about all of us. He's never felt more scared than he does now. He's never felt we were in more danger.'

'Are we?'

'I don't know.'

I doubted I would fall asleep, but I did at last. When I opened my eyes it was the middle of the night. I've no idea what woke me. General nervousness, I think. I lay there for a while, listening to Jenny's small movements. Walter was still outside, circling the hut in his measured way. That reassured me, and I dozed off again. The next thing I knew a few more hours had passed and there was a hand on my face. I sat up, unable to see who it was.

'Jenny?' I wondered.

It was Walter. 'There's s-something wrong,' he said. He knelt next to me. He didn't look calm – though his hands moved lightly onto my shoulders, as if he was trying to keep *me* calm.

Helen was awake, too.

'What's going on?' I whispered.

'Let Walter show you,' Helen replied in a voice she had trouble controlling. 'It's OK. Don't get scared. Just let him show you.'

Jenny's arm was draped across mine. I didn't know if she

was awake until she said, 'Here,' matter-of-factly. She plucked at my right hand, lifting the fingers up to where the back of her head would be.

'N-no,' Walter told her quickly. 'Not y-yet, Jenny. The top first.' Walter gave me one of his smiles. Not a real smile. He was obviously trying to prepare me for something frightening. With a rising sense of dread, I put my hand on top of Jenny's head. Then I breathed a sigh of relief. It felt normal. I could feel the roundness of it, and the hair.

'Now, s-slowly, f-further down, Tommy,' Walter said.

I glanced at him, preparing myself for a shock, but I wasn't prepared enough. Nowhere near enough. What I felt there made me pull my hand away sharply. It couldn't be right. It felt so wrong that I was afraid to put my hand near Jenny again.

The back of her head was entirely missing.

I could run my hand smoothly over the crown, but there was a gap where the back of the head and neck should have been – like a piece taken out of her. I drew back. I couldn't help it. I didn't want to frighten Jenny but I couldn't keep my hand there.

Walter gave me another pained smile. 'That's n-not all,' he said. It was only afterwards that I realized he'd deliberately asked Jenny to let me feel her head first. He did that to help me adjust. He wanted the first part I touched to feel the least strange.

'It's all right,' Jenny said, conversationally. 'Feel my arms, Thomas. Go on. Feel them. Go on.' I didn't want to, but Jenny insisted. One of them felt normal until I reached the fingers. There was something wrong with those fingers. They felt too soft, as if they would slip away. I swallowed and then moved on to her other arm. The forearm was ordinary in shape, but all over it there was thick matted hair. I shouted when I reached it.

Half human, I was thinking. Oh no. Half human and half something else. I was suddenly glad I couldn't see her. I felt ashamed thinking it, but I still didn't want to see.

Helen had been quietly watching me all this time.

She raised an eyebrow. 'Nothing?' she asked. 'These changes to Jenny don't mean anything to you?'

'Should they?'

'No. I just hoped they might.'

'What's going on? Is this anything to do with the way animals are attracted to her?'

'No. It's something else,' Helen said. 'I think it's what the Protector was trying to tell me about.' She sat beside me. 'Listen, Thomas, the missing parts of Jenny's head and neck are only the beginning of the changes to her. Walter's examined her all over, and there are several bits now that aren't human. She's got some sort of unusual jaw arrangement for a start. And her mouth isn't in the usual place; it's kind of slung under her chin. And she's got an extra limb, with an object fixed on the end that's incredibly strong. It's not a claw, but it's not a hand, either. And she's warm in places she shouldn't be. There's also something on her tummy. It keeps trickling off.' Helen shuddered. 'I've been listening to it. It keeps dripping on the floor. Jenny doesn't know what it is, but … I think I do. At least I've an idea what it could be.'

Jenny chose this moment to stand up. She brushed by me, and I felt the texture of rough skin as she passed. The door opened. Milo cast a strong light outside, allowing me to see Jenny's outline. The new Jenny wasn't girl-shaped any longer. There was a swollen area under her belly. For a second I also thought I saw three eyes instead of two. And there were clusters of spikes where her chin should have been.

Walter followed her out. He wanted to pick her up, but was unsure how.

Jenny shuffled back through the doorway and clambered up his legs. She put her little misshapen head close to his. 'Help me, Walter,' she said – and even her voice sounded different, frailer, as she sang a little rhyme, one of the twins'.

Walter carried Jenny back to the bed. I watched as he felt for the areas of her body safest to touch. Finally he stroked her back to sleep.

Helen sat beside me.

'During the night, Thomas,' she said, 'I thought about the Roar. I thought about her a lot. I always do that, but this time was different. I don't really know what the Roar looks like – I've only had glimpses of her body as she moves through space – but she definitely has some extra limbs, and now Jenny has something like that. And the Roar has thick hair along her flanks. And I think there's poison, too. I was thinking about all those things last night, when I sent my mind out to the Roar.'

'Are you saying that's poison falling on the floor?'

Helen sat at the edge of Jenny's mattress, peering down at her. 'Not yet. She's dripping a liquid, but I think it's harmless because Jenny doesn't know what's in the Roar's poison yet. She doesn't know because I don't know. I know it sounds weird but what's happening to Jenny has something to do with me. That's what Jenny's been asking of me all this time. She's like a mirror. With every thought I have about the Roar's body, she changes in some way.'

'Why? She's not becoming ... a Roar, is she?'

'No, it's not that.'

'Like one of the newborn, then?'

'No. I don't think it's anything like that. If I'm right, Jenny's learning about her enemy.'

'Learning?'

'Thomas, I think she's a weapon.'

I couldn't take that in.

'If I'm right,' Helen said, 'that's what Jenny is. Another defender, if you like. But she needs me to help her. That's what she's asking me for. You gave her your beauty. I've got something different she needs.'

'I don't understand.'

'What's the one place I can go that nobody else can?'

I thought of the Roar.

'Exactly,' Helen said. 'That's what Jenny needs me to do. She's a weapon, but she doesn't know how to be used. She needs to know more about the Roar's body. She needs to know more about the weaknesses of her enemy. I need to show her. I need to go deeper into the mind of the Roar.'

'To find out what?'

'To find out what she's frightened of.'

six

starscape

HELEN

'Could you stay outside, Walter?' I asked. 'Make sure nobody disturbs us. No interruptions.'

He didn't like leaving me alone in the hut at a time like this, but he understood why I was asking and so did Thomas. I stayed inside with Jenny. She was crouched on the floor, waiting. Against the dark earth of the hut floor I couldn't see her at all. Then she rubbed her hand over mine, and I felt a few long alien hairs against my skin.

I shivered, but it didn't matter. The hairs were only the beginning of something that could help us – if I could find it.

'Just me and you this time,' I whispered.

Jenny dropped the dolls of the twins and pressed her little warped head against my lap. There were no birds, insects or animals near the hut. She'd forgotten about them for now. Only this mattered.

'Time to find her,' she said impatiently, pushing my head down on the mattress.

I wasn't so eager. Whatever weaknesses the Roar had, I didn't expect to find any. It had been me who'd exposed *our* weaknesses to the Roar, not the other way round. Everything the Roar knew about Coldharbour's defences, about Milo, even the precarious state of the Protector himself, she'd learned from me. In the early days I'd gone racing inside her mind without understanding the risks or ever shielding myself properly.

Yet the Roar hadn't attacked me. Not seriously, not intending to kill me, anyway. Why? A slip-up on her part? Missed opportunities? I didn't believe that for a moment. The truth was that I'd been much more useful to her alive than dead.

But she *could* kill me. She was capable of it. The deeper I went into her mind the more vulnerable I was. She'd promised her newborn the pleasure of my death, but if I was enough of a threat I knew the Roar wouldn't hesitate.

I settled back on the mattress. Jenny knelt beside me, anxious but excited.

I closed my eyes and thought about the Roar. The last thing I expected was for her to show me any of her vulnerabilities, but she had to have some. She was famished, for a start. She was also at the end of a gruelling journey, one she'd had to consume parts of her own body to complete. And she was no longer young.

Whatever you've told me, I thought, I don't think you're quite the killer you once were.

I kept saying positive things like that to myself, while Jenny interlaced her fingers in mine. Her hands were already warmer than a human's should have been.

Then I felt another, lighter touch, dappled sunlight on my eyes.

The Protector.

'Where will you go, little one?' he asked. Again that laugh, though it wasn't mocking. 'To the Roar? Is that where you would choose? To the killer herself? To one who expects you?'

'Where else?' I thought.

A pause. Then, 'Think differently. Who has roved upon her body? Who knows parts she has never seen? Who fed from the starving regions of her? Who knows her infirmities as well as she?'

I considered that. 'The newborn?'

I felt a silent affirmation from the Protector, a tingle of acknowledgement.

Jenny clutched my arm, suddenly sensing the danger ahead.

'Will it hurt, Helen?' she asked.

I nearly said 'no' the way you automatically do to reassure a small child.

'It might,' I said.

The method I usually used to approach the Roar involved sneaking up in cringing terror to the edges of her mind, hoping not to be noticed. It had never worked, but the Roar knew my style well and that was useful to me now. I made sure that I approached so slowly and warily that even the sleepy newborn sensed me coming. The Roar, of course, knew it was me long before they did. Almost lazily, she invited me in – and, just as she did, I leaped fast into the mind of one of the newborn.

The second newborn. I chose that one. The mistake-prone newborn.

And this is what I found: first, that she was female; in fact, both the newborn were female.

A mother and her two daughters, then.

Easy to think of them that way.

I wasn't stupid enough to let that homely thought take root, though. No mother here. Or not one I recognized. An assassin and her fledglings, more like. A killer and her would-be killers.

Then I made another discovery, and this one surprised me: there was *guilt* in the newborn's mind. I'd expected to find details of hate and cruelty and varieties of death – whatever the Roar had been able to teach her on the voyage – and I did find those things, but mostly I found the second newborn dwelling on the mistakes she had made on the journey here. She was vexed over those mistakes – mistakes the other, slightly older, newborn had *not* made.

All those mistakes, when her mother was so weary.

So weary?

I tiptoed through the newborn's mind for the meaning of that – and found something. Both newborn had nibbled dangerously close to the arteries feeding the Roar's primary heart. The muscle between that and the Roar's secondary heart was damaged. A powerful shock to the area could wound the Roar, possibly kill her.

Beside me, Jenny's fingernails sank into my arm. Her breathing was fast – as was Thomas's. He sat outside, held by Walter, his beauty beginning to shoot into Jenny.

For a moment I hesitated. I almost drew back. Then, calming myself, I sneaked back to the second newborn's mind. How to reach the Roar's heart? The newborn had scampered inside every crevice of her mother's body. She had to know the way. I followed dozens of memory trails, and finally I found it – a path into her mother's body. It was an open patch near the Roar's tail-flukes, where she'd bitten them away on the journey. A small enough object, if it approached unobserved, could enter the damaged area and ride the veins up into the Roar's primary heart.

Suddenly, now that I had the information I needed, my main concern was to slip away without being noticed. I did it stealthily. No sharp tugs.

There was no reaction from the Roar.

Beside me, Jenny's body started to alter. Even before I drew my mind all the way back to Coldharbour, she was changing. Outside the shack, I felt two things: Walter holding Thomas up, and Thomas himself clenching his fists with the effort to control his beauty.

Jenny took it. She plucked a huge new tide of beauty from him, and despite everything he had given before, this was a new test for Thomas. Milo had once taken as much, but never like this, never so fast. Jenny ripped it from Thomas without consideration. There was no intention to hurt him. This was simply more important.

Walter pushed open the hut door to discover what was happening, but I warned him back.

I was next. I knew that. Jenny would take what she needed next from me. I could see the outline of her eyes. They gazed into mine and it was terrifying that she could demand so much. I braced myself. I thought that by knowing what was going to happen, I'd be able to endure it better than Thomas, but it didn't make any difference. Jenny's eyes dilated, and something ripped knife-like into me, seeking everything I'd discovered about the Roar.

Then Jenny transformed utterly. I saw her outline. It was no longer the outline of a girl, or anything like it. Any clue that might have alerted the Roar to Jenny's presence – any smell or hint of humanity – was gone. She stood up smoothly. Her body was a black void. No, not entirely black. A blackness dotted with bright points.

Widely spaced dots against a velvet background.

Stars, I realized. A starscape – the same starscape the second newborn was seeing as she travelled through space.

Camouflage. Faultless camouflage.

There was a moment of regret from Jenny, as if she finally understood what all of this meant. Then even the outline of her face disappeared, followed by her neck and shoulders. Her first transformation had been into something like the Roar, a way to teach herself about the body of our enemy. This time Jenny was something entirely different – a weapon for killing. Her body thinned. She became slender, torpedo-thin and moist. The moistness was important: it would enable her to travel as freely and easily up the Roar's arteries as the Roar's own blood.

Jenny floated out of the hut. I knew exactly how she would come within reach of the Roar. She would approach as a backdrop of stars, undetectable. She would enter through the veins and only when she was inside the Roar's body, too far inside for the newborn to root her out, would she cling to the muscle of the Roar's heart and slice it apart.

What would happen to Jenny afterwards? I hadn't thought about that. I had no idea if she could return, or how.

But Jenny did not hesitate. She drifted upward. Against Milo's silver, she could be seen easily, but I knew the Roar would not see her.

Jenny glanced skyward, wanting to go there.

'Wait,' said a voice. The Protector.

I hesitated – and so did Jenny.

'A fragile heart?' the Protector queried in the lightest of voices. 'Too human to be the weakness of a Roar, Helen. Only human hearts can be attacked so easily from the outside. A Roar has a dozen defences for it. She has tempted you with something you would easily understand.'

I raced back to the Roar, and found this: her avidly waiting. Not for me. Of course not for me. For Jenny. Willing
her to come after her. I'd been misled. There had been no
mistake from the second newborn. This time the newborn
had done her job well. The Roar, suspecting I would go
there, had invented a weakness for me to find.

It was all lies, a trap for Jenny. If Jenny had gone to the
Roar in the form I'd given her, she'd have been killed.

The Protector said, 'The Roar has played such games for
longer than you, that is all. She is a consummate assassin.
She knows a trap is best set when the prey sees its chance.'

'I can't afford to make mistakes like this,' I thought desperately. 'Help me. I'm endangering everyone!'

Again the touch of sunshine. 'No, you have not done that.
I would not have allowed such a mistake. Not every decision
should be questioned, especially when you, so new to it,
have only begun to question.'

On my knees, I staggered from the hut. Outside, an exhausted Thomas was pressed against Walter. As soon as Walter saw
me, he picked me up as well. Jenny gradually floated back
down to the ground. By the time she touched the soil she
was a girl again. The starscape was gone, the slender shape,
the moistness. I wasn't surprised. How could Jenny be a
weapon when my insight was meaningless? She tottered in
dismay across the mud, rubbing at her normal arms in dis-
gust, as if she still had a memory of hair. A few birds flapped
around her, but she ignored them.

Walter lifted her up, and she curled up against his neck,
pressed her whole shaking body into him. She didn't even
look at me. Thomas did, though. He'd been through so
much to give Jenny the beauty she needed, and now he wondered if all that beauty had been wasted. He wondered if

he'd have to give that much again. He couldn't imagine doing so. He didn't want to say that to me, but he was thinking it.

Finally, Walter covered Jenny up and took her back to his hut.

I returned to the shack and collapsed on a mattress. Thomas followed me in.

'Not now,' I murmured. 'Please. Leave me alone, will you?'

'I'm not here about anything to do with Jenny,' he said. 'You've been so preoccupied you haven't even noticed, have you? When was the last time anyone heard a scream from the Roar?'

'What?'

'I'll tell you how long it's been. Not since Jenny started to change into that star-thing. They've stopped! The Roar's screams have stopped.'

It was true. I'd been too distracted to realize. Throughout Coldharbour, children were already whispering about it. Letting my thoughts drift amongst them I discovered something I hadn't felt for a long time: hope; a small ray of hope. The absence of the Roar's screams was such a small thing to pin hope to, but already it was spreading. No one said anything too openly yet, because it seemed impossible to believe that the Roar had simply – what? Stopped coming towards us? Given up?

'Is it … gone?' a girl outside whispered. 'Isn't it coming any more?'

Her words hung in the air, and I didn't want to say anything to break the spell they created, but I had to. A little respite? What had we done to earn that? Surely Jenny's failed attack hadn't frightened the Roar off.

The Protector was quiet, though I sensed he knew the

answer. Again, he was teaching me.

'Let's see,' I said.

I closed my eyes – and immediately opened them again.

'Walter!' I threw open the shack door, and he was beside me in seconds. 'Stay with Jenny!' I told him. 'The Roar knows she's dangerous now. No matter what happens don't leave Jenny's side, not for a second. Do you hear me?'

'Helen, what's wrong?' Thomas demanded. 'Why are you shouting?'

'The Roar hasn't gone,' I said. 'She just doesn't need to scream any more. Now she's arrived, there's no reason. She's *here*.'

Seven

weapons

THE ROAR

The Roar hovered near the Earth.

How could this have been so easy? she wondered. How could anything as large as she catch them by surprise? In the final surge of speed across space the only precaution she had needed to take was to avoid casting her immense shadow across the Earth.

These children, she thought. So easily frightened. So inexperienced in battle. They had never been forced to defend their world before. A few inconsequential screams was all it took to send them into panic. They were no threat at all.

She surveyed the vastness of her body. On the journey through space the threat of starvation had forced her to eat her tail-flukes and some of her lower limbs. Much of her speed-musculature had also decayed. Had she been confronting a Protector in its prime these losses would have been devastating, but this world's Protector was clearly no longer a threat.

How remarkably naïve of Helen to have revealed that so easily! An astonishing mistake.

The Jenny child posed a different kind of challenge. The Roar had not seen her like before. An adaptable weapon, obviously. Best to kill her quickly. A pity the trick of enticing Helen with the second newborn had not worked. Nevertheless, the inexperienced Helen would clearly make further mistakes. Any one of those would enable her to destroy Jenny.

The important thing now was to defeat the silver child.

He was the main threat.

Isolate and kill him.

The Roar flexed her body. It was still firm, still taut. True, three of her lungs had not re-inflated after the ravages of the voyage, but her teeth were intact and her hearts pumped away with all their former characteristic vigour. The main setback was the damage to her clench-limbs. Most were still usable after the journey, but the fifth hung withered and useless. Without it, there would be no easy way to launch a final deadly strike against the silver child.

Well, perhaps Carnac, when he emerged, could act as the fifth clench-limb. He could pin Milo down with his bulk. Yes. That would work. It would also be good for Carnac to know *he* had delivered the last blow to execute the silver child. That way he would get a taste of killing at a younger age than even she had.

All the best assassins started early.

But what about her more delicate weapons? Had they survived the journey? Warily, the Roar opened out her various blocks, blinds and thread-rapiers. The thread-rapiers were minor assault weapons, not much use against a Protector, but effective against a smaller opponent such as Milo.

The design of the silver child's body was bizarre. It presented almost an embarrassment of targets. The lungs, especially, and also that single woefully frail heart – how easily Helen had been convinced a Roar's heart was like it! But there were endless other flaws to this human frame as well. The throat. The eyes. The hinge gap between the ears and the jaw. And a skeleton easily snapped; all those brittle segmented bones. The base of the spine, in particular, was vulnerable, and the neck vertebrae.

Thanks to Helen, the Roar knew all about those neck vertebrae.

And the nasal passages. The curious holes of the nostrils. Straight lines up to the brain. Unusually, there was no intervening bone to guard the brain itself.

A thread-rapier could easily penetrate it.

The Roar weighed the balance of forces. During the voyage she had seen no more Protectors. That was her main concern now, not these children, or the enfeebled Protector below, but a fresh Protector on her trail. She had not detected any of their tell-tale silver tracks, but how could she be certain?

Her newborn, sensing their mother's concern, became still and anxious.

'No need for that,' she told them. 'Roam freely over me.'

They did so, scurrying across her face and playfully biting her skin. It had been an arduous voyage for them. They had known only the passing of stars and the gradual consumption of their own siblings.

The Roar had no choice about that – to avoid starving she had been forced to eat all except two of her newborn. One of those, her strongest, had enjoyed the challenge of staying alive. The second newborn had not. Throughout the journey she had lived in fear, nervously comparing the size of her jaw to those remaining, and always, always pushing the weaker newborn closer to the Roar's eyes, so she would see them and consume them first. When the last few were left, she had changed tactics. She had stayed quiet. Sometimes the second newborn had stayed quiet for centuries, hoping not to be noticed.

Now that she had arrived over the Earth, the Roar let both newborn relax. She enfolded them gently in her clench-limbs, making them feel safe. The second newborn was in high spirits after the deception of Helen, and the Roar let her brag on. There would be no further punishment for past mistakes. Now, on the eve of battle, the newborn must be focused and sharp. She offered both, at long last, the complete acceptance again of their mother.

'Time to decide how we will overcome this world's defences,' she said to them.

'Use the poisons!' clamoured both newborn.

'They are not yet sufficiently potent for the silver child.'

'When will they be ready?'

'Soon.'

The newborn begged to be shown, so she let both scuttle into the four sac-glands of her abdomen and watch how she mixed the poisons in greater and greater concentrations.

Following this, she reviewed all her old battles with them. The newborn had a fondness for one particular encounter – the first time the Roar had fought alone against a mature Protector. That Protector had been a large female; the Roar had been young and not yet its match in strength, but females know some things about one another, even across the divide of species, and the Roar had recognized what would frighten the Protector most – she had gone straight for the female's child. First the child, to distract the mother.

Then, when the mother was unbalanced and terrified, the mother itself.

No one understood the power of that strategy better than the Roar.

Her newborn, reminded of it, felt strangely uneasy.

'Name all of our weapons,' the Roar ordered.

She listened patiently as they called out her full armoury. The newborn were in a hurry to use everything, of course, but the Roar knew better than to deploy her finest weapons straight away. Why waste energy? Her first attack on Milo, if carefully planned, would reveal everything she needed to know.

'And you also have us,' the strongest newborn told her proudly. 'If your weapons are not enough, you can use us to strike the smaller targets.'

The Roar noted the courage of the offer, but had no plans to risk either newborn in the upcoming battle. Except at the end, of course. Except for Helen and the loved ones. She had promised them that. Warm glows came from the newborn as she reminded them of it.

'The silver child,' she said. 'A new nature of enemy. How should we defeat him?'

The newborn were full of suggestions, each trying to impress her, but they had no experience to draw on. The Roar only half listened to them as she considered her options.

Milo was certainly aware of her. The Protector had been feeding him information for some time about the strategies of a Roar. The classic assault skills she would normally deploy against a new opponent would probably be ineffective against him. She needed to come up with something different.

'Milo is not a mother,' her first newborn suggested. 'But

… is there not a child? Why not attack the blood-relative? Attack Jenny, the younger one. The one he cares about most. Distract him that way.'

The Roar was pleased to hear this. How satisfying that a newborn should come up with such an idea. Deep in the Earth, even Carnac softly murmured his approval.

So the Roar set her newborn the task of finding a way to kill Jenny, while she pondered the threat posed by the rest of the children.

An odd species, she thought. So small. So easily alarmed. Anything I do is likely to terrify them.

There were sudden nips and bites near her mouth.

'We see him!' both newborn squealed. 'We see the silver child!'

The Roar's three eyes followed their gaze. Milo was clearly visible in the northern hemisphere of the world. On a planet covered by light clouds, he looked like a glossy, burnished patch. To the south of him a blue-grey ocean covered a quarter of the world. After the darkness of space, its vivid colour excited the newborn. The Roar's olfactory and other scanning glands automatically evaluated the planet for food. For most of the voyage her digestive systems had been inactive, but the pain from her newly awakened stomachs was now almost unbearable.

It was tempting to attack Milo immediately, but it made sense to eat first. There was plenty of food on this world. The majority of it was swimming, flying or running towards the silver child, but not all. The plants were rooted, and some of the animals were too slow or ill or distant to make the journey to Milo, no matter how much they wanted to reach him.

The cold southern ocean regions, she thought. A vast rich source of marine food was there, all of it too far from the silver child to be shielded by him.

Yes, she would start in that place.

She projected her sifts forward. The sifts were slender sucking tubes that could be extended quickly from the lining of her digestive tract. For this small world she needed only the thinnest ones.

Both her newborn, hardly able to contain their excitement, crawled into her stomach. There they waited, while the Roar extruded the sifts. She looped them under her jaw and dropped them towards the planet.

sifts

HELEN

I was inside the shack when the first thoughts from the Antarctic animals reached me. It wasn't fear they felt initially. They were wary, that's all. A few were even curious about the vast new structures that stabbed into the freezing waters.

Sifts. Somehow, from my time in the Roar's mind, I knew their name.

The first two broke into the ice floes of the Weddell and Bellingshausen Seas. They trawled the murk of the bottom, then rose up to the more promising surface waters. Feeling along the fringes of the pack ice, they began sucking in thousands of tons of plankton and krill.

When tiny, simple creatures die there is not much fear – they don't have any true dread. Most don't even know they're dying.

Birds are different. Startled by the eerie winds stirred by the sifts whole colonies of shearbills and skuas were taking off from islands all across the southern ocean. The penguins, being flightless, didn't stand a chance. Millions of pairs of Chinstrap, Crested, Adélie and Rockhopper penguins on Ross Island, South Shetlands and the Scotia Arc were taken almost at once. The Emperors, largest of the penguins, huddling together within the snows of the Antarctic interior, survived only a little longer.

The wave of fear spread by the birds reached the animals. The only ones left were those that had been too ill, too young, too old or far away to begin the journey to Coldharbour when Jenny's call came. With whatever strength they had left, these animals now fled for their lives. Fur seals and walruses left their beach-head perches. Fish sought protection in shoals. The remaining whales did what they had always done in times of danger: in an attempt to escape they dived deep.

There was nowhere deep enough to escape the sifts.

I couldn't take in death on this scale. I kept focusing on one group of animals after another, unable to pull myself away from the horror of their destruction.

'Helen! Will you listen!'

It was Thomas, yelling in my ear, but I barely heard. In the south of the world, flock after flock of Dominion gulls were leaving their young behind, making a dash across Drake Passage. At the same time albatrosses were battling over the Amundsen Sea, trying to reach the Argentinian coast. I couldn't tear my thoughts from those albatrosses. With their powerful wings they were just managing to resist the reverse winds of the sifts, but behind them shorter-winged fulmars and sheathbills barely made it from their island coasts. The last one, a fulmar, died in great surprise, never understanding what had happened to it.

There was another bellow in my ear, followed by a sharp

tug on my shoulder this time – Walter after my attention. I shrugged him off, staying with the albatrosses.

Then Thomas slapped me on the arm, and the shock of it brought me back to Coldharbour.

'Helen, will you *look!*'

'Get off!' I shouted.

'Then listen! What's the matter with you? We need to know what's happening!'

He hauled me from the shack and made me stare up.

Above us, Milo was poised to depart. Ever since Jenny had stopped glowing his view of the world had widened. It wasn't only the creamy patches of children that he saw now. He saw animals almost as fiercely. He saw their terror across the world.

'Is Coldharbour under attack?' Thomas demanded. 'If so, we need to get word out to the child-families!'

Milo's whole body trembled. His wings faced southwards. I knew how much he wanted to leave. Like me, he could see all those deaths in Antarctica. The only reason he didn't fly there at once was that he knew the sifts would drop down on us if he did.

But Coldharbour's youngsters were frightened. Seeing Milo tremble, many started to run towards the Barrier, trying to reach their parents. The leaders of the better organized child-families were attempting to get them back under cover, but it wasn't easy. At the Barrier itself there was chaos as parents themselves surged forward.

Dad, I thought. He was caught near the Barrier edge. All around him adults were pushing forward, forcing him to lean dangerously. If he fell over now he'd never get up again.

I followed him. For several minutes I followed him, and then he fell. A tiny woman reached down to help him up before he was trampled. At last, together, they broke away from the worst of the crowds, escaping northwards.

Thomas was still screaming at me. Then I heard him yell, 'Walter, just take her inside! Take her into the shack!' and the next moment an arm picked me up.

Even after I knew Dad was safe, I couldn't focus on what was happening in Coldharbour. I didn't care about what was happening in Coldharbour. No one was dying in Coldharbour. Across the southern oceans they were all dying. Then I thought about another ocean.

'The twins,' I whispered.

That silenced Thomas.

I sent my mind out to the western Pacific. Emily and Freda were thousands of miles from the sifts, but the shock-waves buffeted them even there.

'Emms?' Freda was saying. 'Can yer feel that? What is it?'

'Dunno. Maybe it's the Protector breaking free.'

'No, no. We'd know if it was. It's something else. If – '

'*Let them go.*'

It was the Protector's voice, cutting across the twins' thoughts.

'Let them go, Helen,' he insisted. 'Do not dwell with Emily and Freda. They are safe. Let them go.'

But I couldn't. I couldn't let the twins go. I couldn't even let the birds go. The albatrosses were still resisting the sift-winds. They had almost made it to the Argentinian coast. If they could reach it there was a chance of wedging themselves into the cliffs, but they were tiring. I stayed with them. I knew it was crazy, but I felt as if I was the only force of hope keeping them alive.

'Let them go, Helen,' the Protector said again, more forcefully this time. 'If you cannot let them go, greater tragedies will be unendurable. There is no hope for them, unless their wings can bear them up. You must accept that, as I have done. For while you dwell on them, you cannot be elsewhere. You are needed in Coldharbour.'

'The twins ...'

'*I* will safeguard the twins.'

I still couldn't leave the albatrosses. I couldn't.

For the first time the Protector's voice was stern.

'Then I will show you something to make you forget the birds.'

The Protector moved my mind to a house near a shore. Two people were there. I hadn't thought about people near the sifts. There were no children left in this remote part of the world – all of them had at least come some distance towards Coldharbour – and most adults, even those without children, sensing the arrival of the Roar, had followed them.

A few remained.

An elderly couple were inside the house.

I had a terrible sense of foreboding, but allowed myself to be led by the Protector. The man and his wife, who was too sick to travel, had woken on Campbell Island, south of New Zealand, to a strange whirring of the air in their room, an unseasonable cold.

Arm in arm they stared out through the net curtains of their upstairs bedroom window at the storm rising up off the sea towards them. The man's wife was asking for her glasses, fumbling for them. Her husband, from some instinct, knew that it was too late for them both. The Protector made me watch as the man clutched his wife with sudden tenderness, trying to get her to ignore the glasses, to look at him.

'Do you see now?' the Protector asked. 'Do you see why you must not dwell on the dying?'

He let me come away, and I lay on the floor of the shack, covering my face.

'Who is not drawn to the last moments of any life?' the

Protector murmured. 'Yet you must not be, Helen. When the Roar attacks Coldharbour she will attempt to distract you by endangering those you love, not strangers such as these. Do you not understand that yet? Do you think the Barrier, when it moved, took your father idly? Do you think the Roar would take an interest in a single man for no reason? She knows: while you watch your father you are not looking elsewhere. Look now. Look at what Jenny, Thomas and Walter are doing.'

I uncovered my face. Through the shack door, I saw Jenny. Her eyes were dilated, almost white. She held tightly onto Walter, gripping him as if nothing else mattered. Then her irises moved sideways. 'More!' she shrieked, clutching wildly at Walter's hair, but it was someone else she meant – Thomas. He shuddered, his chest banging off Walter's knee from the effort to control his beauty. Even so, Jenny demanded more from him, and more again. And as she took it wolves at the borders of Coldharbour howled as if this was the onset of winter.

'No!' Walter shouted. 'N-not the animals, Jenny.'

'But –' She waved her arms frantically.

'No! Just the birds.'

He wrapped his arms around her, and he was right to. It was too much for her to control all the animals and birds at the same time.

The flocks burst from Milo, rising to defend us.

'Slowly,' Walter said – and Jenny did exactly that, aligning all the flocks at the southern border of Coldharbour, until they faced in the same direction as Milo, just beyond his wings. It took her a long time to get the last flocks airborne, and the effort to keep them aloft meant the pupils left Jenny's eyes entirely. They were blank and she lifted them like a blind person might lift them to the sky.

But she couldn't help the Antarctic birds. Even with Thomas giving her his beauty, Jenny couldn't reach that far. She tried. Sensing their fear, as confused as the dying birds themselves about what was happening, she tried to draw as many towards Coldharbour as possible.

If Jenny could do that, I could at least gather myself. I did so. I put the albatrosses out of my mind. I told the others what was happening. Then I sent word out to the child-families and, though it took time, an uneasy calm slowly returned to Coldharbour. The crush at the Barrier also eased off. Dad was safe, for now at least. Jenny and Thomas, incredibly tired, lay slumped across Walter, and I stayed with them, trying to push all the death from my mind. I didn't go back to the south of the world. The Roar was still actively feeding, so I wanted to find out what was happening there, but I didn't. I stayed away from the albatrosses. Either they had out-flown the sifts or they were already dead. I couldn't do anything for them now.

In fact, I realized, I never could have.

Jenny slept for an hour or so, but that's all the sleep Walter allowed. He woke her, determined after what had happened to speed up her efforts to control the birds.

'I'm tired,' she moaned, pushing him away. 'Leave me alone!'

'You c-can sleep later.'

He carried her outside the hut. Gradually, reluctantly, she brought all the flocks under control, but when she yawned, dropping her arms, Walter made her raise them again and continue. For the rest of the afternoon he challenged her to improve her control over the birds, sometimes playfully, sometimes with an edge in his voice. And I encouraged him. We both knew that unless he pushed her to the limit the birds would never be ready for the arrival of the Roar – and even then they might not be.

In the evening, Jenny joined me in the shack.

I didn't need to tell her about the albatrosses. Her mind was now linked to every bird in the world.

'It's all right, Jenny,' I said, putting her on my lap. 'It's not your fault.'

'Isn't it?'

'You couldn't have done anything.'

She rubbed my arm softly back and forth, as if she was the older one, and I the little girl who needed comforting.

'Will they all die, Helen?'

'I don't know. Most of them will.'

'They didn't know what it was. The birds and the animals didn't know. They didn't even know why they were dying, did they?'

I stroked her hair. 'No, Jenny, they didn't.'

I couldn't help myself then – I let my mind drift back to the Antarctic. Before I reached the albatrosses I felt the Protector's presence, warning me away.

'How can you stand so much death?' I wondered. 'How can you?'

'Because you must,' he answered. 'You learn to. You think you know now about death, Helen? If you were older, if you had embraced more of life, you might understand, perhaps.'

Suddenly he projected an image into my mind.

I saw planets and star systems. I saw the silver bodies of the Protectors. I saw the Roars surrounding the Protectors' planet, and several others.

'The Roars arrived from another galaxy,' the Protector said. 'They were starving when they came, and at first we willingly shared our food. But they demanded more than that, they wanted whole worlds, and when they began to maraud and scavenge the planets of the outer galaxy, we had no choice except to fight if we were to defend those worlds. But the Roars always bred more quickly than us, and were our equals in strength and, though we held them back for many ages, finally they established the assassin-teams, and after that they hounded us without pause. In the end, we sent the strongest surviving Protectors to encircle the Roar home world, so that they could not return to their breeding grounds, but even that failed. One by one the Protectors were killed by the returning assassin teams. I would not wish you to see a murder at the hands of an assassin-team, Helen,' the Protector said. 'I would not wish any creature to behold such a death.'

I waited for more, and finally the Protector said, 'And yet all is not death. Life will find a way to survive if it can, even against the dominion of the Roars. Some animals escaped the sifts, and are heading towards Jenny while she sleeps. The Roar thinks only of taking life, Helen, but life holds on where it may, and as long as Jenny's thoughts harbour them there will still be hope for creatures that would have had none.'

Nothing more came, then I felt a shiver through the sunlight dapple.

'Milo will not be alone in the battle ahead,' the Protector said. 'With what energy I have left, I will confront the Roar with him. But I am half-blind and I cannot fight both her and Carnac together, not without help. They defeated me in another age, and I am weaker now than then. The Unearthers must hold that fight for us.'

'The Unearthers?'

'Yes. A great deal depends on them now.'

I sent my mind deep beneath Coldharbour, where the Unearthers, under Tanni's leadership, sweated in their tunnels. Carnac was close to them. For days he had been steadily easing his way up from the liquid rock and heat of the Earth's mantle, towards the crust.

'How long before he reaches the Unearthers?' I wondered.

'Carnac is already in position,' the Protector replied. 'Now that the Roar has arrived, he merely awaits her signal to begin his move against them.'

Nine

drills

TANNI

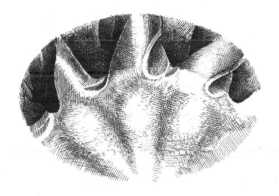

'How long have we been down here, Tanni?' Parminder muttered.

'How long does it feel like?'

'A year. No, more like *ten* years.'

I raised my free drill-hand. It wasn't really a hand. It was a huge blob of steel, fingerless and circular, with metal drill-parts all around the edge. Thomas had strapped a handy luminous-dial watch to it just before we'd left Coldharbour's surface two days ago. I checked it.

'Forty-three hours,' I told my drill-partner.

'You're joking! It can't be only that long!'

'It is.'

There were one hundred and ninety-eight of us Unearthers. Here we were, four miles under Coldharbour, cringing in the dark, lying in wait for Carnac.

Even those words sounded absurd now. *Waiting for*

Carnac. As if he was a pal of ours, instead of a monster intending to kill us!

It seemed like an age ago that we'd agreed to return to the lowest drill-tunnels to become the first line of defence against Carnac's attack. But the sun had been shining on our backs when we made that decision, and we'd all been fresh-full of hatred for what Carnac had done to us.

Keeping our nerve down here in the dark was proving harder than I expected.

Our carbide-and-diamond-impregnated drill-hands no longer functioned efficiently. They still rotated – if we all attacked at the same time, I was sure they'd give Carnac plenty to worry about – but without Thomas's beauty powering them they couldn't cut through rock any more. We'd had to lower ourselves very carefully down the same tunnels our drills had previously carved out in no time.

Past Second Camp, into the far drill-depths and the sweltering heat.

Looking back, at least that journey down gave us something positive to do. Once we reached the lowest tunnels, there was nothing to do except wait. We couldn't even see each other properly. Torches had been strapped to our heads before we left the surface, but the batteries had run out long ago, and the bronze glow-faces Carnac had given us only gleamed dully now. Outside of a thin bronze halo we cast there was utter darkness.

All the Unearthers were attached together in the same way as me and Parminder – drill-on-drill, inseparable. 'Partners for life,' as Parminder noted dryly. 'You realize that, Tanni? They'll never separate our drill-hands. I hope you like me. I hope you like me a lot.'

A sobering thought.

I had no idea how best to deploy the Unearthers to fight

Carnac, so I stuck to the previous team structure: each team was a group of eight, composed of four linked pairs. Wherever possible, I kept the old drill teams intact, but I decided to break up the younger teams. I was worried that at the first hint of Carnac's approach they'd bolt up the nearest tunnel to escape. I couldn't take that risk. So the oldest paired children in each team were now responsible for a younger pair. It worked – sort of. At least no one had run away yet.

We'd all been waiting, crouched side by side in the lowest drill-tunnels, for over four hours now.

'Well, this is certainly fun, Tanni,' Parminder said in her best deadpan voice. 'Oh yes, I like it down here. A real holiday camp. Hot enough for a tan. I'm glad you persuaded me to stay.'

It was just Parminder grumbling, but she was right about the heat. It had gradually built up during the descent. Half the food we'd brought had already gone rancid, and had to be eaten or chucked away. We were nearly out of water, too. I was really worried about that. Metal throats and lips don't get as dry as normal ones, but we still needed to drink something.

Parminder's bronze face shone next to mine.

'Show me those lovely metal teeth of yours,' she said.

I grinned obligingly.

'They're truly stunning,' she said. 'Gorgeous, in fact.'

I told her where to go.

There'd been an edgy banter simmering between us for hours. Nervousness made all of us gabble on and on. The subject didn't matter – any old drivel was better than nothing. Given the tension, I wasn't surprised how popular anyone who could raise a laugh became. The best joke-tellers, like Parminder herself, were almost treasured. She'd actually invented a whole new category of jokes. Unearther jokes, she called them. Jokes for metal heads. Every half an hour or so she'd come out with a new batch. A half-decent one and we'd all be cracking up, exploding with nerve-filled laughter.

The biggest problem, of course, was the waiting. Every tiny little sound down here became magnified. Someone would accidentally breathe in your ear, and your heart would slam into overdrive. So I kept thinking up distractions to keep everyone's minds off Carnac. Anything to keep us busy. Like short sprint tunnel races for the youngsters. Or sharpening our drill-hands on the rocks around us.

I also reminded everyone about the Barrier, that there was no going back to mums and dads. Cruel of me, perhaps, but I couldn't afford any sentimentality. We'd all agreed to come down here. Even if I'd discovered the Barrier was gone, I'm not sure I'd have let the others know. I was determined that we'd be the first line of defence against Carnac.

If I had to tell a few white lies to achieve that I would.

As the hours passed, some of the more frightened team members started to pretend that Carnac wasn't coming up after us at all.

'He might turn up outside Coldharbour, further out to sea.'

'He might not know we're here.'

'He might miss us on the way up.'

I even heard this: 'Carnac's hurt us before. He won't do it again.'

And this: 'If we stay quiet, he won't hear us.'

I could have tried to stop these barmy conversations, but I didn't, because we had to talk about something. Anyway, I wasn't immune to my own brand of wishful-thinking. The youngsters were the best at it. They had a wonderfully endearing habit of finding hope. They latched onto every crumb of it the older Unearthers chucked at them. One little girl became convinced that by simply closing her eyes she could keep Carnac away.

She practised it. Her drill-partner did the same.

We sat around, forever discussing our chances of survival. It was weird, because none of the older Unearthers really believed we could live through Carnac's attack, but that didn't hold us back. Oh no! We needed to believe we had some kind of chance.

Parminder summed it up like this: 'We can't hold onto anything with our drills, but we can cling onto Carnac. Sort of hook our drills in, then ride up on that big body of his to the surface. And if we're fast, and bury ourselves inside him, we can wait there. We'll be under his skin, protected from the rocks above. He'll reach Coldharbour – we won't be able to stop him doing that – but all the while we'll be burrowing into him, driving him insane, doing our part for Milo. And when Carnac emerges, if he's near the ground we can just climb off. But even if we fall, so what? Our bodies are pretty tough. We can survive a big fall like that.'

When happily-ever-after conversations like that petered out, Parminder would give us whatever new jokes she'd thought up recently. 'OK, try this one,' she'd said a few minutes ago. 'Why wouldn't they let the little Unearther boy with the metal ears go to school?/Don't know/Because he was hard of hearing/OK, what kind of music do Unearthers like?/Heavy metal/ Right, an Unearther kid barges in to the doctor's ...'

And I'd think, good or bad, keep it up, Parminder, keep it up.

But we needed more than jokes to keep us going. What we needed was a plan to deal with Carnac. A plan which gave everyone a task to do and also a plan simple enough for the youngsters to follow.

Having no idea how to best fight Carnac, the one I devised kept us as flexible a fighting force as possible. I didn't want everyone dependent on me giving orders. I might be the first to die. I didn't say that out loud, but I thought it. Every drill team had to be able to act on its own. So I gave each team responsibilities. I appointed a leader, and a deputy-leader in case the leader became hurt. The leaders' duties were to keep a listen out for Carnac and, if they heard him, get their team members' drills pointing down at the floor as fast as possible – oh, and offer some final words of encouragement.

The encouragement bit gave me a few problems. For some reason all the team leaders expected me to come up with an inspirational line. I said I'd get back to them on it, but they kept pushing me. What I finally said was, 'Just tell your team this: anything we can do to stop Carnac, or slow him down, will help Milo. That's what we're here for. To help Milo. Feel proud of yourselves.'

It sounded a bit lame, I'll admit, but I couldn't come up with anything more impressive, and for about an hour afterwards various girls and boys amongst the team leaders were practising those words in whispers. Privately I wondered if we'd get any real warning about Carnac's attack. He'd probably just lunge out and smash us in two seconds. Eat us, maybe. A nice little morsel.

I didn't say this to the other leaders, but they weren't stupid. Some were definitely having similar thoughts.

I decided on the drills-down position because I thought it was most likely Carnac would attack from below. If I was right, it made sense for our drills to be the first part of our bodies he reached. After that we'd dig for all our worth, use our drills any way we could to get inside him. I had no idea if we could do that; I just hoped.

Pretty soon even the smallest team members had mastered getting quickly into the crouch-down posture. I made them go over that part the most. I wanted to ingrain it completely into their heads.

And do you know something, practising this way seemed to help. We worked well together, we weren't so frightened, and there was less talk of Carnac not coming. I was beginning to get almost comfortable with our new routines when one of the team leaders shouted, 'I hear something!'

Beneath us, there was a noise – a thick bursting rasp, like an abrupt loss of pressure.

For a second it was possible to believe that it wasn't Carnac. Then there was an almighty rending of the rock below us. I was glad to see several drill teams immediately checking off with each other, names being barked out, drills dropped to the floor. Other teams were paralysed by fear.

'This is it, isn't it?' Parminder murmured.

I stood up, hauling her with me, and shouted at the top of my voice, 'All drill teams into position. You know what to do! Get into position! Hands down! Hands pointing *down*!'

For a minute or so there were no more sounds from below. Good, because otherwise I'd never have restored order. I crept with Parminder along the lines of teams, trying to keep them focused. Many people were crying – and not only the youngsters. Eventually I had everyone at least shakily pointing their drills down. Some team leaders had started encouraging their members.

'Feel proud of yourselves … feel proud of yourselves …'

Then – suddenly – another huge explosive noise from below.

Each of us fell silent, listening for more.

It came again, a long boom, followed by scraping. I didn't look at the others. I didn't trust my face to have the right expression in that moment. Then the noises ended. Nothing. We waited, listening, crouched down, our backs beginning to ache, our shaking faces casting bronze light over the tunnel walls.

Five minutes.

Two more unbearable minutes, and I knew the drill teams couldn't stay in their state of readiness. Carnac was just below us, but we couldn't remain in this rigid downward pose. It was too awkward a body position. We had to relax from it, but how? We'd never practised an orderly stand-down. It had never occurred to me that we'd need it.

'All right,' I called out as calmly and clearly as I could. 'Sit back everyone. Get out of the drills-down position. Leaders stay alert.'

A barrage of questions flew out from the teams.

While I answered them, I also listened to what was going on under us.

Still nothing from Carnac. Why? Was he toying with us? Or could he be nervous about attacking us? A ridiculous thought, but for a fraction of a second my heart leaped with hope. Then Parminder brought me back to reality.

'He's probably waiting,' she suggested. 'He's close to the surface where he is. He can break out easily any time he likes from there. He's waiting. Waiting for the Roar to give him a signal. When she's ready to launch her attack, that's when he'll break through.'

Yes, I thought. That's right. When Mother gives him the call.

I hadn't planned for this, and a whole range of emotions swept through me. There was relief not to be fighting, of course. But as the minutes drew on, and it became obvious that Carnac wasn't going to attack, I grew more and more desperate. This wait was the last thing I wanted. We couldn't afford to wait! We had virtually no food or water left. And now that the others knew how close Carnac was, there'd be no more jokes. We'd all be cringing in terror until he made his move.

I'll have to keep the drill teams on permanent alert, I realized.

But I couldn't do that! They were too scared. I'd have pandemonium in no time if I forced them to. And what about the team leaders? There was already enough pressure on them. If I put any more on their shoulders, I knew I'd have a rebellion on my hands. I couldn't afford that. If just two or three of the team leaders refused to do what I asked, the rest would quickly follow.

I couldn't see a way out of this. I needed Carnac to attack at once. He had to! In that moment, it was insane, but I wanted nothing more than for Carnac to attack and have done with it! If I'd had a knife to prick his hide, I'd have poked him.

'It's all right,' I said. 'It's all right.' I murmured that over and over to myself like a pitiful mantra. I didn't even know I was doing it.

'Shut up,' Parminder hissed. 'Everyone can hear you.'

I did shut up, but not before at least half a dozen others noticed what I was doing.

'Oh no,' I heard one girl say. 'Tanni's losing it! He's losing it!'

Ten

emergence

THOMAS

Helen's news to us about the Roar's devastation of Antarctica spread rapidly among the child-families. By nightfall everyone in Coldharbour knew and by dawn next morning more than twice the usual number of visitors were following Walter everywhere.

Jenny, with Walter by her side, kept encouraging the birds from far-flung distances into Coldharbour. It was an incredible sight, an endless stream of exhausted-looking flocks gliding in hour after hour, making for the safety of Milo. There were no decent places left to roost in Coldharbour, of course, so they took their chances, landing wherever there was an inch of spare mud or shivering against the low hills to the west. 'Anywhere,' Helen told me, 'as long as they can still see Milo and stay close to his wings.'

Coldharbour's children, meanwhile, anxiously watched the sky.

Everyone, that is, except Helen.

The deaths in the Antarctic were still going on and, although she mumbled that she was coping fine, all morning she locked herself up in the shack. She only came out now and again to give me the occasional message to pass on to the news-starved child-families.

In the early afternoon she emerged again. She'd had a quick wash and tried to freshen up before seeing me, but it didn't make much difference. She still looked terrible. Straightening out her hair with a nervous tug, she said, 'If I'm that bad you'd better come in.'

She made room for me on her mattress. Food brought in earlier by Walter was untouched on the floor. 'Nothing's changed,' she said. 'There's no sign of the Roar's feeding coming to an end. If anything, the sifts are spreading out northwards into places with more people.'

'People? What's happening to them?'

'I don't want to talk about that. I … can't.'

I waited, then said, 'When's the feeding going to stop?'

'The Roar's preparing for battle. I think she wants to gorge herself before taking on Milo. She might not stop until there's nothing alive left in the southern world. Or she might stop at any time. I just don't know.'

'Have you been back to her mind?'

'No.' Helen smiled grimly. 'After what the Roar did before, I didn't want to give her any more advantages.' She opened the door, obviously wanting to be alone again. 'I know everyone's scared,' she said. 'When there's better news, I'll let you have it.' I thought she was going to let me go, but as I turned to leave she suddenly put her hand on my shoulder. 'What about you?' she asked. 'I know it's been hard, the amount of beauty Jenny's taking.'

'I'm not worried about that.'

'Oh?'

'There's plenty left, Helen. More than enough.'

I'd been feeling it all morning – a build-up in the level of my beauty. I'd even tried heading off into Coldharbour again, hoping to find someone to trigger it, but Walter wouldn't let me leave. Now that the Roar was here he didn't want any of us straying far from the shack.

'I've got more beauty inside me than ever,' I said. 'It just needs – I'm not sure – I think it needs – '

'Somewhere to go?'

'Yes.'

'And you think Emily and Freda will know who can use it?'

I glanced up. It was always unnerving when Helen picked up on your thought before you had time to say it. 'Yes,' I said. 'The twins have always led my beauty to the children needing it most.'

Helen stared thoughtfully at me for a moment. Then she walked across the hut. She came so close that her shirt brushed against me. For some reason I almost expected my beauty to reach out to her.

I whispered, 'Why don't you take it?'

'I've … tried,' she said self-consciously. 'Once … when I visited the Roar. I thought it would help.'

'And?'

'Nothing. I don't think your beauty's meant for me, Thomas.'

'Isn't it? Are you sure? That's not what I've felt recently.'

Helen sighed. 'I think that's more to do with what's happening to you than me. Your beauty's changing. We're all being drawn to it. I'm not sure why, but one thing's for sure: everyone's asking after you. They're all talking about you. And watching you.'

'Watching me?'

'Haven't you noticed?'

As I left the shack, I saw what Helen meant. Whispers and odd, furtive looks. Children glancing weirdly at me, as if I was some kind of long-lost brother or freak. I had no idea what it meant.

'Hey, Tommy.'

It was Walter. I could just about make him out through the birds buzzing around his big shoulders. All morning they'd been attempting to perch on him, but he didn't seem to mind. With great dignity he simply shooed them off.

He stood near the shack, surrounded by his visitors, surveying Coldharbour with those mammoth eyes of his. He'd acquired a new weapon as well – a steel girder. It was twenty feet of solid metal and must have weighed half a ton. When Walter wasn't doing anything else he had an unnerving habit of tossing it casually between his hands.

Jenny was snug inside a special fur-lined pouch tied to his waist. Walter had made it so that he could free up his arms and still keep her beside him at all times. If I'd given him half the chance he'd probably have stuffed me inside there as well. He didn't like me wandering.

As soon as he saw me leave the shack his long arm reached out, yanked me up by my jacket collar and hoisted me up onto his shoulder. He always did that if I got close enough. His visitors stayed nearby, staring enviously up at me. Walter shuffled his feet. He gave me old lopsided. I think he was trying to look smooth and charming.

'You need to stay c-closer to me, Tommy,' he said gravely. 'You wouldn't have to g-go in the pouch. You c-could just sit on …' He wasn't sure what I should sit on. He moved the girder to show me his knees.

'Mmm,' I replied. 'Tempting. Jiggle up and down there, shall I, keeping the girder company? Yes, really tempting. I'll stay near the shack, Walter, but I'm not spending all day and night tucked up beside you. Jenny might not mind, but I do.'

'Thomas?'

'Yeah?'

He rubbed his fingers along the edge of the girder, his face suddenly serious. 'Thomas?'

'What is it, Walter? Spit it out.'

'Look at m-me.'

As I turned to peer up at him, he cupped my face in his hands.

'Listen to me, Tommy. Are y-you listening?'

'Yes,' I said, swallowing.

His grip tightened, his face perspiring mildly.

'If I'm k-killed …' he said. 'If I'm killed, I've told my v-visitors what to do. If I'm s-stopped or c-can't defend you, they will. Do this one th-thing. If anything h-happens to me, s-stay with them. They know the defences better than you. They'll protect you. With their l-lives, Tommy. Do you hear me? With their lives.'

I met his gaze with difficulty.

'That's too much to ask, Walter. If they've agreed to it, it's only because *you* asked. And it's not fair to ask them.'

Walter pulled me towards him. There was no smile. 'You d-don't understand, Tommy. You matter more than they d-do. They know that. It's your b-beauty. Without it, there's no chance for them. If you d-die, so will they.'

I couldn't find a reply to that. For a while we both peered out across Coldharbour, saying nothing.

'You won't be killed, Walter,' I said, more to myself than him. 'I don't know why you said that. You won't die. You survived the Unearthers. If they couldn't kill you –'

His finger gently covered my lips.

'The Roar's n-not like the Unearthers. You know that, Tommy. I'm a d-defender, like Milo. The Roar w-will come after the defenders first. If anything happens to me, be r-ready, that's all.'

His hand closed around the back of my head and I gazed at the visitors. They surrounded us. Most looked frightened. 'They won't feel the same way about sacrificing themselves when they see the Roar,' I whispered.

'No, they w-won't,' Walter said. 'But they'll d-do it any-way.'

Jenny had been listening in on all this, and she gave me one of her quiet little smiles. A shy smile. Her eyes had a slight dilation to them – a sheen – and my beauty, noticing it, simmered with subtle expectancy. I smiled unsteadily back, and together the three of us watched the afternoon sun rising over the northern rubbish dumps of Coldharbour.

'Are you ready, Thomas?' Jenny asked a little later.

I didn't know what she meant. I thought she meant for the big challenge ahead, whatever it would bring, but I was wrong.

She'd noticed a change in the wind coming in off the sea. Quietly the change started, so quietly I barely noticed it, but Walter was on his feet in a second. Jenny's dress rustled as she pulled herself out of the pouch. At the same time she raised her arms, and flocks of birds took to the air.

Something was coming for us. At first it was just a dark rumble at the sea horizon, but then we saw it – a wave. A vast wall of water. It reared up to obscure the sun, ten or more times the height of Walter.

Jenny's birds did not hesitate. They flew straight towards the danger.

Like everyone else, I looked at Milo.

Who was tensed. Whose gaze was on the sea. Whose silver wings were fully extended.

Walter immediately grabbed me and Jenny and sprinted towards the shack. At the same time Helen ran out, staring towards the coast. Walter snatched her up and searched for the safest place to take us.

Across the sea, the colossal wave approached. As it reared up towards the beaches I knew that Walter could never outrun it. Only Milo could stop it smashing into Coldharbour and drowning us all. We expected him to drop his wings. When he didn't, Walter was unable to decide where to go. Even his deepest tunnels would be flooded by the wave.

He faced north and began to run.

Jenny sent out half the birds to meet the wave, but what use would they be against it? Just beyond the surf, the whales and sharks rose up, mouths open, knowing they could not stop it either.

'No!' Helen shouted. 'Don't you understand?' Her face was exultant.

Walter pushed her head down, but she resisted him, peering at the sea, her hair flying straight back in the wind.

It was hard to see the wave clearly. There was a huge amount of light behind it – a huge amount of approaching silver in the sky. And then something reached through the wave, from the heart of it.

Whatever it was, it was immense. The only thing I could compare it with was a mountain, but how could a mountain move like this? In any case it was too wide to be a mountain. It covered the entire south-eastern horizon. It dwarfed the long stretch of Coldharbour Bay.

'Are those fingers?' I shouted. 'They can't be.'

'Like fingers,' Helen replied breathlessly. 'But more complex. Better than our hands, Thomas! More flexible. The Protector calls them *Evissas*.'

The mountain-sized object approached across the sky. Each of the digits Helen had called *Evissas* was attached to an enormous wrist-like structure. There were fifteen of the Evissas on the end of that wrist, and they were somewhat like fingers, except each was the same size, and more dexterous than fingers, curving and weaving across the clouds as if they could mould themselves into anything they needed to be.

I watched, mesmerized, while the Evissas shaped themselves into a definite object – a final form. And then the fifteen digits thrust through the oncoming wave. The whales and sharks, seeing them, dived to safety. Birds, commanded by Jenny, drew back as with incredible force the Evissas came to rest against the sea bed, a short distance from the beach. Each Evissa folded against the next. Without gaps, like a shield, they formed a barricade around Coldharbour. A mountain-hand.

And then a voice boomed, 'Do not be afraid.'

It wasn't Milo's voice. A lighter voice. It didn't match the size of the Evissas. A gentle voice. It made every child in Coldharbour stop.

The next moment the wave crashed against the mountain-hand. There was a long drawn-out shattering of water as the force of the wave collapsed and subsided harmlessly. Then the Evissas slowly parted. Between them I could see a huge area of silver-white flesh. It extended for an impossible distance across the sea. A limb, I realized. Not an arm, though vaguely like it. A limb the size of a country.

'The Protector,' Jenny murmured.

Across Coldharbour there was a gradual hush. No one was shouting any more. In the sky, the edges of Milo's wings trembled. The birds, released by Jenny, soared overhead or gazed out to sea. And what we saw next made us gasp.

The Evissas opened, and something from inside them tumbled out like grains of sand into the shallows.

The ocean-children.

We watched as they slipped in their thousands from the Evissas, climbing down onto the land. For a few minutes they lingered in the flesh and the waves near the beach, clearly not wanting to leave the Protector's embrace. Then they ran towards us. Those on the shoreline reacted at once, then child-families from across Coldharbour were heading in the same direction to welcome back relatives and friends.

And all the while the Protector did not speak again. It did not speak, though I wanted it to.

'When we're ready,' Helen told me. 'He's waiting until we're ready.'

'He?'

'Didn't you hear a male voice when the Protector spoke?'

'No,' I said. 'It's more like a woman's, isn't it?'

Helen smiled. 'I think we each hear what will reassure us most. What we need to hear. A woman or man. Some hear a child.'

All across Coldharbour there were tearful reunions. Afterwards, blankets were brought out, clothes, anything dry and warm, as everyone offered what they had to the cold and weary ocean-children.

Two, however, were missing.

'It's OK,' Helen said. 'You'll see. Emily and Freda don't want to leave the Protector, that's all. They know they might not get a chance to be this close to him again.'

It was mid-afternoon when the twins appeared at last.

They didn't run like the other children, of course. They were much faster than that, scurrying on all fours as always, that unique insect-like scuttle. Tossing their red hair, they scampered along on the tips of their nails so fast that I could hardly follow them.

'Who first?' I heard Emily hoot at Freda.

'Thomas first!'

'No! Helen! Or Jens!'

They laughed, and then said together, 'Walts!' and the next moment they launched themselves, burying their heads in his shins. Emily slapped a kiss on him and grabbed his face.

'If I'd a pin, I'd flick it!' she cried, bending his hair in all directions.

'If I'd a pound, I'd nick it!' Freda yelled, rubbing his bony cheek. She planted a wet kiss on Jenny, then turned to me. 'Not embarrassed are yer, Toms?' she asked. 'If I do this!' She laughed as I just avoided grazing her lips, then caught me properly after she'd hugged Helen.

Finally, with tears in their eyes, and both looking incredibly tired but happy, the twins slipped away into the shack to change out of their sodden dresses.

Walter joined them in the shack. He'd had a change of clothing waiting for them for days. No dresses, though. Even Walter couldn't easily obtain those. I listened outside as the twins sized up their new garments.

'Got these from yer visitors, I bet,' I heard Emily mutter, sniffing the clothes. 'Not bad. Clean, anyways, but how're we supposed to run about in trousers, Walts, and what's *this*?' He started to apologize about the clothes, but she stopped him with, 'What happened to your jacket and shoes? Get in another scrape, did yer, or you just been busy? Never mind,' she said quietly, as he tried to explain, 'we'll soon 'ave you fixed up again. There's time for that now. Shush, what you doing, what's the matter with yer? What yer doing that for? There's no need for that. We're all right. We're fine. Come 'ere to me. It's all right.'

A little later they emerged from the shack. Walter came out first, proudly carrying a girl in each arm. He put them down and sort of patted their heads. Freda glanced at me self-consciously. She was wearing a long-sleeved cotton shirt. Walter had also picked out for her a wide-brimmed felt hat, pointy-toed shoes and corduroys.

Emily had on a brown polo-necked jumper, but Walter had managed to find her a hat just as tasteful as Freda's. It was brilliant. It was one of those black leather ones, with the funny flaps that fall over the ears. She tucked the jumper into a pair of blue denim jeans that were at least a size too big for her.

Trousers on the twins: I'd never seen anything like it, and I burst out laughing.

Freda gave me a withering stare, and then she saw the entrances to some of Walter's underground defences.

'Gawd, we're away five minutes and look what you done to the place!' she groaned at him. 'What're they doing there?'

Walter smiled, showing them the easiest way to clamber down. The twins nodded and made a fuss over the defences as if they were deeply impressed, but I could see they didn't fancy the earthy smell of them too much.

'Suppose it's an improvement o' some kind,' Freda said as convincingly as she could.

'Yeah, yer can go down ... for ages,' Emily added, clutching onto Walter's arm. 'It's ... good.'

'What's this?' Freda asked, sticking her thumb into Walter's pouch. When he told her, she whispered privately to Jenny, 'Wiv nothing to do but scrunch up in there, you must

'ave been bored though, eh?' Jenny nodded. 'I bet Walts did-
n't let yer get out, either, did ee?' Jenny shook her head. 'Ee's
like that,' Freda said. 'Once ee gets hold of yer, yer never get
away from 'im.' She gave Jenny a sly grin. 'So, what's all this
I been hearing? You been changing, Jens, Toms says. Weapon
or something. D'yer mind?' She gingerly touched the back
of Jenny's head. 'Feels all right to me. Needs a wash, though.
Been too long up against Walter's filthy jacket, ain't yer. Ee'd
never think to wash it. Don't worry – we'll soon sort him
out.'

Jenny smiled up at her happily.

Walter, though, was beyond ordinary happiness. The six
of us together again! He couldn't wipe the smile off his face!
The twins were hungry, and nothing could have pleased
Walter more than the task he set himself for the rest of the
afternoon, that of kneeling beside them, spooning stuff into
their mouths. But Emily stopped eating for long enough to
take me aside and say, 'We'll 'elp find that child Helen says
you been looking for, Toms. We'll just 'ave a rest, then we'll
find whoever it is.'

Walter trotted in and out of the shack for the rest of the
day with endless snacks, until finally the twins convinced
him they'd had enough. Then Freda insisted on closing the
door of the shack on the rest of the world, and looked us
over. 'Well,' she sighed.

About an hour later a party of Walter's visitors rapped on
the door, laden with even more food, and this time the six of
us ate together. Afterwards, Emily thanked Walter for the
jeans, and then asked, only when he had a moment to spare
of course, if he'd look for something 'more suitable', to
which he agreed.

For his part, Walter showed the twins Jenny's pouch, and
indicated, only half-jokingly, that it wouldn't take him long

to make it roomier or create a new one specially for them.

Finally, wanting to make sure the shack was properly protected, he excused himself and went back outside, plucking a few of his visitors at random from the mud to spend time with. But even with his visitors he looked lonely out there, so we joined him. The twins hung off his arms, peering uncertainly into the dark holes of the tunnels. Helen clung to his waist. Jenny crept into the pouch and I, for once, sat on Walter's knee and pretended to enjoy it there. At least twenty more visitors sneaked up his legs as well and, with Walter swaying a little under the combined weight of us all, we sat back to watch the afterglow of the sunset fade over Coldharbour.

We stayed together until nightfall. It was the brightest, most luminous night I could remember. There was Milo, of course, shining as always, but now there was a new light source as well. It glowed from somewhere out at sea, overshadowing even Milo's radiance.

I looked for the cause of it. Everyone did, drawn towards the silver glow over the waves. Sometimes it shone steadily on us. Other times it flickered up to the sky like a search beam, lighting up the clouds and every detail of Milo's wings.

'It's an eye,' Helen informed us. 'The Protector's eye. It's half blind, but it still sheds light.'

'Blind?' I said.

'Carnac and the Roar did it to the Protector during their last battle.'

I gazed out over the waves.

'But where's the rest of him?'

'He's withdrawn to the ocean. His muscles have wasted away. He can't stand yet. He's too heavy. He has to let the ocean take his weight for now, though at least he's in the shallows.'

'How big is he?'

The twins grinned, poking my arm.

'Ee's lying across two oceans, Toms,' Freda said. 'Only his head and one arm is in our sea. That's all we saw, anyways. Oh, wouldn't yer love to see the whole of 'im?'

The night passed slowly, and each of us except Walter retired to the shack. I was too excited to sleep, though. There were no more screams from the Roar, so I should have tried harder to catch up on what I'd missed, but I couldn't relax. Finally I got up and went outside. Lots of others were awake as well. More awake than sleeping, in fact. Whole child-families gazing solemnly out to sea. And then, I'm not sure what time it was, the Protector spoke to us.

I knew he was going to speak. Just before he did, I knew. And I suppose it should have felt odd, hearing a voice without seeing a mouth, but it didn't. I wondered for a moment if the Protector was speaking different languages to all the children at once; then how he was communicating with us didn't matter. Only the tone. Not even that. Something deeper.

'Wake, if you have not done so,' the Protector said. 'Tender is the weight of your sleeping breath, but there is little time left now for sleeping.'

There was a pause, while the children of Coldharbour not already up were roused. Then the Protector spoke again, and his next words were ones we had all needed to hear for a long time. 'I am your Protector,' he said, 'and, now that I am here, there will never be a time again when I am not with you. Never.'

He said a lot more to us that night, though if I'd been asked afterwards exactly what I couldn't have recalled it all.

I'd expected a feeble voice, after so much injury, but the Protector's voice wasn't feeble. There was no weakness, but there was no false strength either. If we were promised anything I don't remember what it was. But I do remember the last thing the Protector told us.

'The light you see burning in the ocean is only the beginning of me,' he said. 'I am your guardian. For each world, a guardian. To each world, a Protector. For the smallest, to be cherished no less than any other. This is not my first duty, and I have never failed before. I was here at the moment life on your Earth began, and I will be here as long as it lasts, and that will be for much longer than the Roar dreams. The fear-creature you know as the Roar is merely an appetite. It knows nothing else. Pity her, especially this one, for though she can think only of death you are strong enough to survive against her. I will be with you. And, if Jenny will command the animals, they will also be with us to the last.' Suddenly there was a burst of unexpected laughter from the Protector. 'The warmth of your sun!' he marvelled. 'Oh, you cannot know what it feels like to experience its touch again! Part of me is on the opposite side of your world, where it shines, and although there are no children to adorn my Evissas there that is because they are with you, or will be. Before the Roar attacks, I will see all children safe under the charm of Milo.'

The Protector said nothing more, and I barely had time to think afterwards before the twins were pinching me and telling me to climb on board Walter. 'What's wrong?' I asked, holding on tightly as Freda made him run.

'You'll see!' Emily hissed.

Walter hurried all five of us down to the beach, where one of the Protector's Evissas was still in the surf. Led by Emily, we swam out until we reached it.

'Come on, Toms,' Freda urged me. 'What yer waiting for?'

She and Emily clambered forward without hesitation and rubbed their noses and chins up against the Protector's coarse skin. It smelled strange: of salt, of course, after all that time under the ocean, but another smell as well, entirely alien. I stole cautiously from the water and put my hand out to feel the Protector. His skin was surprisingly warm.

My hand against a mountain.

Walter then took a turn, running his palm along a broad length of the Evissa. Some of his visitors, who had followed us, ventured from his side to press themselves up against the Protector or sprint across the sand on the beach near to it.

Jenny and Helen were content to stay on Walter's back and watch the rest of us, but the twins wouldn't have it, and hauled them twenty or thirty feet up the rough skin-surface. I think they'd have dragged us all the way to the top if the Protector himself hadn't warned against it. Afterwards, Helen told me the Protector had only left the Evissa on the beach to give the twins a final chance to say goodbye, goodbye at least until the battle with the Roar was over, and who knew what would remain of the Protector then?

There was a slight tremble, a gentle reminder that the Evissa was about to be removed – enough time for each child to understand and climb back down. Then the mountain was withdrawn beyond sight, and only the silver of the eye remained far out at sea to remind us of what we had just touched.

Eleven

a child to catch a child

HELEN

Over the next few hours we took care of the twins.

Typically, they wanted to begin searching at once for Thomas's special child, but it was obvious how much they needed rest and, despite protests, Walter carried them inside the shack and placed them as carefully as broken-winged birds onto their mattress. Their eyes closed before he'd even covered their shoulders.

Sweet dreams, I thought.

It was always wonderful to watch the sleep of the twins – face to face, their slender pointed chins touching. On this occasion, though, you could see the toll the ocean had taken. Their normally vivid freckles were barely visible, their lips grey, their skin bleached bone-white. Emily's face in particular remained pinched and screwed up, as if she was still trying to hold out against the pressure of the sea.

Walter, placing another blanket around their necks, tiptoed to the front of the shack to watch over them with me.

'They'll recover,' I told him. 'They need rest, that's all.'

Emily had kept her jeans on for extra warmth. One of her legs stuck out from the blankets.

'She looks s-strange in those, d-doesn't she?' Walter murmured.

He was right. The jeans made Emily appear smaller. Younger, somehow. More vulnerable. But at least she had the consolation of marvellous dreams, because she dreamed about the Protector. All night she and Freda dreamed about the affection he'd shown them under the sea, and for hours I stayed secretly and greedily in their minds, wishing I'd gone down with them.

'Do you wish it?' The words came like a thrill as morning approached, followed by a speckle of sunlight. 'You envy the twins their time with me,' the Protector said, 'yet the relationship we have, even from this distance, is closer. You are a revelation, Helen.'

'A revelation?'

'To have mastered so swiftly the mind-skills the Roar and I required a lifetime to master. Your entire species is unique, startling, touched with fledgling destiny, but it is above all others you, Helen, I am in wonder of.' He was silent for a moment, and I sensed what was behind his silence.

I thought, 'You're frightened for us, aren't you?'

'Yes. If I could remain in these shallows I might recover to protect you better, but the Roar's attack will be soon now. I have given Milo all I can. He has the best of me, and when the battle is underway I will bear him up for as long as I am able, but it may not be enough.'

I sensed the weight of responsibility the Protector felt. He was reluctant to give more of that to me – though I also sensed he had no choice.

I said, 'I need to go back to the Roar's mind. I know that. I know I've got to do a better job of finding her weaknesses, so Jenny can become the weapon she needs to be. But how? The Roar just plays her games. Every time I'm with her she discovers things about us she'd never know without my help. And I'm useless. Whenever I get inside her mind, that's what she wants; it's always a trap.'

'Yet she is afraid of you.'

'Of me?'

'Why do you think she dallies now at the edge of your world, Helen? Not merely to feed. And not for fear of me. It is because she has never encountered an opponent such as you or Jenny. When the Roar allowed animals through the Barrier, it was because she never recognized that they could be a threat. She made a mistake with that, and now she cannot stop Jenny bringing them. It unnerves her. The Roar hesitates. A warrior all her life, an inscriber of pain, yet she hesitates.'

The Protector flashed an image of the two newborn at me.

'I hate them,' I thought.

'Do you? Hate them, because their mother chose the path of the assassin?'

'They'd kill us if they could.'

'Death takes many forms, Helen. Perhaps we can use their eagerness for it.'

I didn't understand.

'Each newborn,' the Protector said, 'seeks to impress her mother, to make her proud. Both these newborn have waited many of your lifetimes to prove themselves in battle. They want a first kill. They desire it. Carnac, already a taster of my blood, is beyond reasoning with, yet I still have hope that the newborn will not follow the path of their mother.

When the battle commences, they will be caught up in the fray, probably killed, unless we can prevent it. And even if we cannot, our best chance is to lure them down to us. For then the Roar will delay her attack. She will negotiate for their lives. She will not want to lose them.'

'Lure them down to us? How?'

'They are young. What attracts the young?'

I could sense the Protector felt uncomfortable with what he was teaching me, but he taught me nonetheless. He had no choice, I realized. He had to ask such painful questions, had to make me understand.

'To draw a child out, Helen, what would you use?'

'I don't know.' And then I did. Of course I did. Another child.

A child to catch a child.

Jenny.

I felt the sorrow of the Protector, almost as if I had discovered the truth sooner than he would have wished.

'If there was a choice other than Jenny to entice the newborn, I would take it,' the Protector said.

'What about me? Aren't I a better target?'

'I knew you would select yourself, Helen, but anything exposing you would attract too much curiosity from the Roar. She might sense the trap.'

'But Jenny's – ' I nearly said, 'only five', though what difference did that make here?

'No, you are right,' the Protector said. 'Being so young themselves, the newborn take a natural interest in Jenny for exactly that reason. But they know also that she threatens the Roar. If we can place Jenny somewhere distant from my Evissas, an area the newborn believe they can reach her, tempt them to act, to try to kill her, we may bring them down to us. But I cannot guarantee this will work. In attempting to capture the newborn, I will do what I can to shield Jenny, but I may fail. Do you understand, Helen?'

'She could die,' I said.

'Yes. I will raise an Evissa in readiness for the assault, and Milo will be forewarned, but the newborns may surprise me. However, that is not what I meant when I asked if you understood. I meant that if Jenny dies it will be worse for you than for her. It will be worse because you asked her to do this, and you did so knowing she is too young to fully understand what risk she takes. And it will be worse for you for another reason. For if she is killed, you will experience not only her death but all the reverberations of that death in every child in Coldharbour who witnesses it. For you, there will be no escaping every consequence. Do you understand?'

'Yes,' I said.

But the Protector knew I didn't really understand, and he waited, giving me a little longer to accept what he was telling me. I felt closer than ever to the Protector in that moment of waiting. Even so, I yearned to be closer still. I wanted not just these conversations, but to go deep inside his thoughts so that I could know everything about him and the other Protectors. I tried to.

His next words were stated gently, but they didn't sting any less for that. 'I would allow you in, Helen, but the Roar is an adept: our defences are few enough, and she might learn the last shreds of my guile from you. But know this at least: there is no further need to go into the Roar's mind for now. In fact, you must not – or the plan will be revealed.' He waited, then he said, 'Jenny should go as far from Milo as possible. Too near his wings and the newborn will be afraid to attack.'

'But who will go with her?' I thought. 'It's too far; she'll get lost. Anyway, I can't ask her to go alone.'

I sensed the Protector waiting for me. He knew what

choices I needed to make, but he wanted me to make them.

'There is only a single brief opportunity to attract the newborn,' he said at last. 'If you had to choose a companion to sweeten the target, who would it be?'

And I knew, of course.

Emily. Freda. Thomas. Walter. All or any of them. They'd been constantly in my thoughts. The Roar knew all about them through me, and so, therefore, did her newborn.

'Walter,' I thought. 'Who else is there, if the newborn get past you and Milo?' I pictured Jenny and Walter walking away from us. I knew I could ask Walter, but I didn't know if I could ask Jenny.

'Helen,' the Protector said, 'do you think I would risk her if there was another way? You must understand: if we do not tempt the newborn down now, in this short period before the Roar herself attacks, there is little hope. And know this: my Evissas will protect two as easily as one. I will leave you to consider the choices.'

A final sunlight dapple, and the Protector was gone.

I opened my eyes. Next to me the twins were still asleep. I didn't want to wake them, but I did. Thomas and Walter knew at once that something was wrong. Jenny crawled from the pouch and stared trustingly up at me.

'I need to ask you something, Walter,' I said.

'Anything,' he replied.

So I told them all, and instead of questioning me this happened: Walter and Jenny accepted the task almost immediately. I'd expected more doubts at least from Jenny, and it's true her gaze faltered when I explained that she would be the main target of the newborn, but not that much. She didn't really understand. As soon as she realized that Walter would be with her, she accepted.

It was the twins who surprised me.

'If it's our only chance to capture a newborn, ain't four targets better than one?' Freda asked. 'Well?'

'Or five,' Thomas added. 'Western Coldharbour,' he said. 'That would be the best place to go. The Barrier there is furthest from Milo's wings. It's behind his legs, so it would take him a while to turn round. Yes, we'd be more exposed in western Coldharbour than anywhere else.'

He cleared his throat. 'I have to go anyway, Helen. Someone's out there waiting for my beauty. I've got to find them. Western Coldharbour's about the only place I haven't wandered much around. With Walter's protection, and Emily and Freda with me ...'

'I know,' I said. 'Yes. Go. It makes sense.'

'But it means leaving you here alone.'

'Me or Emms will stay wiv you,' Freda said.

'No,' I replied. 'I'll be nearer the Protector than you, within range of his Evissas. Anyway' – I attempted a smile – 'if the newborn get past the Protector, I don't think it'll make much difference who's with me. Thomas needs you more than I do. Find his child.'

'We will,' Emily said, lowering her eyes.

'How b-big are the newborn?' Walter wanted to know.

I couldn't answer that. I only knew they were large.

'W-what if both n-newborn attack at the same time,' he asked. 'If one attacks us, and the second attacks y-you here. What then?'

'Then either they'll both be stopped or some of us will be killed. Or all of us.'

Walter breathed heavily. Then a smile cracked open on his face, and he was suddenly seeking the right words, his big eyes drinking me in. I wondered why, until I realized it was in case this was the last time he ever saw me.

'If I'd a smile like yours,' Emily said, holding him, 'what'd I do?'

'I'd smile all day long,' Freda said, 'and care for it, too.'

'It's all right, Helen,' Walter said solemnly, 'I'll t-take care of them.'

I nodded, but I couldn't even take comfort from those words. I wanted to believe that Walter could take care of everyone, but how could he? Could he outrun a newborn? Maybe if he was alone. No, not even then, I thought. As for Thomas and Jenny, they wouldn't stand a chance. Nor the twins. I'd seen them in the past move with a speed Walter himself found difficult to match, but there was virtually no strength left in those thin legs after their ordeal in the ocean. They might manage a short sprint. After that, they'd have nothing left.

'Leave as soon as you can,' I whispered.

As part of final preparations Walter spoke privately to his visitors, and hundreds of them set out in every direction across Coldharbour on a special task. He asked his most trusted and capable visitors to remain with me. Less than an hour later he led the others away.

The early morning sun was high in the sky behind Milo as Walter set off. Emily and Freda had switched back into their old dresses again, for freedom of movement. Jenny bobbed up and down inside the pouch.

Jenny. Our little five-year-old weapon. Everything had been explained to her, and she'd agreed to leave, but how could I have imagined anything like the sight of her waving to me as I sent her off to what could be her death?

Walter took a last look around, then squared up his shoulders and headed west. It was a strange leave-taking. None of us said goodbye. I don't think any of us dared to. Usually the twins gave you a peck on the cheek – always some kind of kiss, even if only making a quick trip to the tips! – but not this time. None of the visitors Walter had left with me tried to follow him. I thought they would, but they did exactly as he asked and remained near the shack.

'We're coming back, Helen!' Emily said fiercely, turning her head. 'We will be!'

There were a few more backward glances from Thomas as Walter led them west, then they were swallowed up in the crowds of children. All except Walter, of course. I could see him for miles, gradually dwindling. He took the girder. Knowing there wasn't much hope of it being useful against something the size of the newborn, he took it anyway.

Finally I went back into the shack and lay down. For some reason all I could think about was Dad. I suddenly wished he was here with me – but, of course, it was better if he was out there as well, presenting the newborn with another potential target.

Dad as a target. I hadn't thought of that before, but I did now.

The day wore on, and for as long as they could see – or pretend to themselves they could see – Walter in the distance, his visitors watched him. Then one of them realized that they'd still be able to see him if they ran to the nearest of the towers, half a mile away, but they didn't go. Instead they watched other children climbing it, sending signals back for another hour or so that Walter and everyone else was still OK.

Towards sunset a group of the smaller visitors asked if they could come into the shack with me, and I said yes.

Twelve

bait

THOMAS

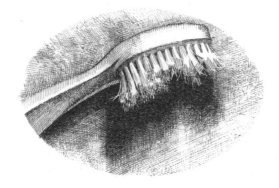

As we tramped across Coldharbour this is what Walter car-ried in a great roomy bag roped to his back: warm coats, endless pairs of socks, underwear, shirts, bottled water, bed-ding and enough food to feed a small army.

His visitors had even donated a couple of battered-look-ing toothbrushes.

When I suggested we wouldn't have time to use those Walter just nudged me higher onto his arm. He was right to bring so much, I suppose. Who knew how long we'd have to wait before the two newborn attacked – if they ever did?

All afternoon we headed steadily west, mobbed by chil-dren. No surprises there – a couple of insect-girls and a giant passing through your territory are pretty hard to ignore! The younger kids did the usual tugging at Walter's trousers to get noticed. Walter's tactic for avoiding this was to crouch down and adopt a sort of blank, straight-ahead stare. It didn't work. They clambered up him anyway. Walter's left arm was like a constantly moving brush, gently sweeping them off his legs. Add to that all the screeching, whistles, warbles and trills from the birds constantly flying over Jenny's head and we were more like a travelling circus than anything else.

At least the newborn won't have any trouble finding us, I thought.

The leaders of the child-families wanted to know what on earth was going on. I concocted a story that we were 'searching for new building materials', but I don't think I fooled anyone.

Several of the child-families started following us. Before long we had dozens trailing in our wake. It was Freda who noticed that most of them were trailing behind me.

'Seen how many admirers you got?' she remarked. 'Pretty ones and ugly ones, Toms. Not just girls, either. Interesting! They've got a strange way o' looking at a boy ...'

She was right. It was the same odd glances I'd been getting for some time now, without knowing what they meant.

'Either you suddenly got a film-star face,' Emily said, pinching my cheek, 'or they're expecting a surprise from yer beauty.' She slipped her hand up against my heart, and whispered, 'What's happening in 'ere, eh? What's yer beauty telling yer?'

'Nothing,' I said.

'You sure? Not even a twinge?'

'No.'

'C'mon, Toms, you're not feeling nothing.'

What was I feeling? I wasn't sure. A slight swirl of beauty? Maybe, but it wasn't strong or active like it had been in the past. It wasn't after a particular child. It just seemed attuned to them all in some way. I told Emily about the time I'd run around eastern Coldharbour, grabbing kids to get them to

notice my beauty. 'They weren't interested then,' I said.
She squeezed my arm. 'They are now!'

But whatever was rousing my beauty hid its secret, and soon
there were other things to think about. Like how far from
Milo we were getting. Gradually we left the protection of his
wings, until only his feet were above us. I didn't like that. I
didn't like not being able to see his face. I wondered what it
was like for Milo as well, forced to watch Jenny disappear
into the west. He didn't turn an inch towards her, but he
must have been desperate to. His little sister, after all, was
being displayed as bait.

I hoped to reach the western Barrier by sunset, but Walter
stopped long before that. He motioned at the low sun, its
rays already slanting into us.

'When w-would you attack?' he asked me. 'If y-you were
the newborn.' I shrugged. Walter put his hand up to cover
the disc of the sun. 'When we c-can't see,' he said. 'W-when
the light's in our eyes, just before the sun sets. B-better stop
now. Make camp here.'

People moved aside to give us a bit of space, and Walter
dumped down all our bedding, clothes and food. He decided against building a new shack, but he did use the girder to
dig out a shallow emergency tunnel so that we could go
there if we had to.

I knew he had other defensive plans as well. He'd brought
two groups of visitors with him, and sent more out east,
south and north before we set off. Throughout the afternoon
those visitors made their way to the towers all across
Coldharbour. When they got there, they began piling rubbish on the tops.

'What are they doing that for?' I asked Walter, but he
merely put his finger over his lips and reminded me to stay

close to the visitors travelling with us, 'Just in c-case.'

He focused most of his attention on Jenny. I think Walter knew better than any of us that her skill with the animals might be our only serious defence against a creature the size of the newborn. He kept encouraging her to work with large flocks, getting her to control their behaviour at greater and greater distances. When Jenny grew tired, and resisted him, he wouldn't let her rest, either; he pressed relentlessly on with the training. Emily didn't like that. 'Stop it, Walts,' she protested. 'Jenny's trying! See the way the birds fly for 'er now!'

Walter shook his head. 'But w-what about when the birds are s-scared?' he asked. 'Will they f-fly for her then? When they see the newborn, and Jenny asks them t-to fly towards that, will they d-do it?'

When sunset approached Walter let Jenny rest at last, held her close and tucked her back inside the pouch. Then he made sure the rest of us were within easy reach, and settled back to observe the skies.

The twins placed a couple of coats out on the mud for us to sit on and we waited. Sometimes we stared at the clouds. Most of the time we shielded our eyes and stared at the sun. I'd never really watched the sun set before. Jenny sat in the pouch, twitching with anxiety. She wore the bright red dress. It looked striking, set off by the rays of the sun. Maybe, I thought, the dress itself will help the newborn locate their target. Then I realized that was stupid. The colour didn't matter. The dress didn't matter. If the newborn knew as much about Jenny as Helen supposed, they wouldn't need a dress flashing in the last of the sun to find her.

It took a long time for the sun to descend. It took forever. When it finally slipped below the horizon the twins and I breathed sighs of relief. Mad, of course – we were supposed to be encouraging the newborn to attack! – but who could pretend they wanted that?

A brisk wind sprang up off the sea. Freda dispensed extra clothing, so we were warm enough, but I missed the shack. It was scary having no ceiling or Milo above us, all that empty sky. I felt incredibly exposed. While we huddled together, I asked Freda if her nose was giving her any useful indications about special children out there.

'Dunno yet,' she said. 'When this is over, we'll find 'em.'

'Them?'

'Me and Emms don't reckon it's one child.' She winked and picked a layer of dirt off my jacket. 'We're sure there's more than that waiting for yer beauty, Toms.'

Twilight arrived, the moon crept up and children headed for the western drop-offs for supplies. Later, a few clouds blew across Milo's feet and he immediately flexed his wings, dispersing them – he didn't want anything obscuring his view tonight.

As darkness fell, he brightened overhead and the twins climbed up on Walter's shoulders, hoping to see that other light far out to sea – the eye of the Protector.

It wasn't there. Submerged. Helen had said it would be – another of the ploys to encourage the newborn to attack. I searched in vain for signs of the Evissas.

Night, and still the attack did not come. The only thing that changed were those piles of rubbish, growing in size every hour on the eastern, southern and northern horizons.

None of us slept, of course. This is when the attack will take place, I thought. In the dead hours. When the newborn think we're asleep. When they can catch us unawares.

Jenny started to get a bit edgy towards the middle of the

night. She was overtired, and irritable, but still wouldn't sleep, no matter how hard the twins encouraged it. I didn't blame her. She didn't fully understand the danger she was in, but she understood enough to keep her awake. The twins, though, knew exactly how to handle our Jenny. Freda had brought their old rectangular mirror and make-up case. Jenny, always wanting to look more like the twins, was fascinated by the whole complicated process as they applied the make-up. She licked her lips the way the twins showed her to make them glisten. Afterwards, they worked on Jenny's hair.

'If I 'ad your locks,' Freda said, 'what would I do?'

'I'd plait 'em and keep 'em,' Emily said, 'and part 'em in two.'

By the time they'd finished, Jenny was all curls and smiles. She hadn't forgotten why we were here, though. The make-up just distracted her. Later, I caught Emily giving Walter's unkempt hair a longing gaze, as if she wanted to tidy that as well.

There wouldn't be time, of course, but we didn't know that then.

We ate late in the night. Afterwards, Freda gave one of the battered toothbrushes to Jenny, and you know, there was something unreal about watching Jenny carefully brushing those small teeth of hers while we waited for the newborn to attack. A quick wash followed – Jenny rubbing her face and neck with bottled water. Then, yawning and finding nothing to dry her wet hands on, she climbed up Walter's arm and wiped her fingers unselfconsciously across his face.

Walter grinned at me – the only grin I'd seen from him all night.

Finally Jenny did fall asleep. Feeling a chill off the sea, I followed the lead of the twins and shuffled closer to Walter.

I couldn't get comfortable, though.

'You're no good at finding the right places on Walts to rest yer head against,' Freda said. 'That's your problem, Toms. Too embarrassed to try 'im out for size!' She pointed out the softest part of Walter's back to lean against, and I propped myself up against the warmth of it.

Walter's back. Like a wall. A great breathing wall.

I stayed in that position, listening out for unusual noises. The only one I heard was the occasional scrape of metal as Walter picked the girder up, put it down again, picked it up, put it down.

First light, I kept thinking. That's when the newborn will attack. First light. As the hours passed, I couldn't shake off that thought. At some point, Emily reached out and touched my face in the completely uninhibited way only Emily could. 'Toms, if you could be anywhere now,' she said, trembling, 'where would yer be?'

I couldn't think of an answer, but Freda, beside me, smiled wistfully. 'If I could be anywhere,' she said, 'I'd be under the sea.'

I was so tired and on edge by the time dawn light filtered into the sky that I almost wished the newborn would attack. At least then it would be over with. But when the attack came, of course, I didn't wish for it at all. I didn't see or hear anything at first – just felt Walter's hand suddenly tighten on mine.

'What are you doing?'

'Something's c-coming,' he said.

I stood up, and the twins joined me. Walter woke Jenny, draped the twins over his knees and lodged me firmly against his shoulder.

'What is it, Walts?' Emily asked. 'I don't see nothing.'

'Can't you f-feel it?'

And then we did – a breeze ruffling our hair. It could have been any breeze, but it wasn't. Walter must have been following the nature of winds across Coldharbour all night to know the difference. He lowered his left hand and drew the now wide-awake Jenny to the edge of the pouch, so she could see. Then he picked up the girder. But when he saw what came out of the sky he lowered it again.

A newborn.

At first I couldn't see her. I just felt the wind rushing ahead of her bulk. She came in near silence, and I suppose that shouldn't have been a surprise. No warning. No roars from this fledgling assassin. Nothing to give away her presence. Only a freshening wind to alert us, and the vibration of her passage across the sky.

Walter shouted a command, and two groups of visitors immediately collected themselves and ran in opposite directions – away from us. A distracting tactic, I realized. Now that the newborn had revealed itself, Walter intended to make it as hard as possible for her to locate us.

The next instant large-winged birds headed towards the piles of refuse across Coldharbour.

It was a signal, if one were needed. Within seconds the rubbish piles on top of the towers were being lit, yellow-orange flames flickering across the dawn.

'Why?' I asked Walter. But when everyone's eyes were drawn to the fires, I knew. Another trick. Another deception. Something to give the Protector a fraction more time to react. Walter's distant visitors were drawing attention to themselves, trying to give us every chance.

Then I saw the newborn, and when I did I didn't believe anything would be able to stop her. She was bigger than any of us could have imagined. She came in from the west, blocking all the light from that part of the sky, and she was almost cube-shaped, except for two thick arm-like growths that slowly protruded from the flattened corners of what appeared to be her skull. I looked for a face, but there was nothing like a face. No features, not even eyes, unless the three polished nubs jutting from her blackened belly were eyes. The newborn extended the arm-growths in front of her broad angular skull. And then we heard her shriek. It sounded exactly like pain and, even in that moment, I wondered if this was the first time the newborn had used the arm-growths, unfurled those weapons, for combat.

The shriek woke the whole of Coldharbour. They all felt the wind and saw the newborn flying level and close to the ground. Everyone except Walter's visitors started running. To my left a teenage girl, leader of the biggest child-family in this area, desperately tried to make herself heard.

Walter stood up – made sure we were securely attached – then stayed exactly where he was.

'What are you waiting for?' I shouted.

'W-where is the other one?'

I'd forgotten about that – the second newborn. I looked around, saw nothing. A single newborn, then, unless the second had gone after Helen. Not that it made any difference to us. We could never outrun anything as fast as the one heading our way. The newborn was still some distance from Coldharbour, but even from this distance I could tell the three forward-facing polished nubs were definitely eyes now. Three eyes thrusting out of the covering of belly-hair.

The newborn didn't deviate. She didn't have to hunt. She came directly for us. The fires made no difference. The scattering visitors didn't confuse her. Despite the distractions, she knew exactly where we were.

'Now!' Walter whispered, and Jenny pulled herself out of

the pouch. Her face was flushed. Her upturned eyes were white. And then she took my beauty. She tore it out of me, and the next moment there was a startling explosion of birds. Walter held Jenny, whispering, keeping her calm, stroking her head, and wherever I looked birds and insects erupted across Coldharbour's skies.

Not towards us. Away from us. Westwards. Straight towards the newborn.

But theirs was slow flight. It was slow, slow flight, infinitesimally slow compared with the newborn's. Even so, seeing the masses of them in her path, the newborn hesitated. Just for a second she hesitated, seeming to ponder this strange new enemy. She paused – lifted her skull, as if smelling the birds and insects – then flew through their ranks.

The birds and insects held the newborn up, but only briefly.

Ignoring their stings and bites, she aimed for us.

We all looked eastwards. Milo was there, but it was a long arc of turn for him to intercept the newborn. And then I realized that the newborn must have calculated this. She had calculated that Milo could not turn in time to save us. Rotating his body, Milo swung a despairing right wing into the west. This fleetingly blocked the newborn, but she slipped deftly under the surface of the wing-edge and came up again beyond it.

For a few seconds the newborn hovered at the edge of western Coldharbour, as if making sure. Then I saw that she did have a mouth after all. Retracted within the head, a fold of skin fell away. A jaw swung down, revealing bank upon bank of layered teeth. We saw the teeth in slashes of motion, as the newborn peeled the skin off them, and again, while she did so, there were those shrieks of pain – as if this was the first use of a weapon or several weapons.

Seeing the jaw, I thought Walter was going to run. Instead, he placed us in the shallow emergency tunnel. Then, standing outside, he planted his feet, raised the girder and prepared to throw. From the entrance of the tunnel, I watched. Some of the faster birds were still following the newborn, harrying her, pecking at her eyes, pecking anything they could reach. But if she felt any pain the newborn did not let that deflect her from her purpose. She was directly above us now, the eyes fixed on us, the undercarriage of her belly elevated so that the arm-growths would have more room to slide and manoeuvre beneath.

Walter held us down with one hand; with his other hand he gripped the middle of the girder like a spear. Then he let go of us, drew his arm back, then further back, altering the angle so that it would strike the softer underside of the newborn, and with a great cry hurled the girder. All his strength went into that throw, and I couldn't believe the speed with which the length of steel went from his open hand into the sky. The newborn was not ready for it. She saw it but not in time. It pierced her deeply and as it entered her she screamed, shaking with pain. Then she reached down, pulling the girder out with one of her thick arm-growths.

And launched herself at us.

Jenny screamed, and with that scream something silver flashed out beneath Milo across the sea.

There were fifteen of them, each the substance of a mountain.

The newborn saw the Evissas – wavered – then came on again. But that was time enough for the Evissas to arch themselves. They formed into a bowl-like shape, glided under the newborn and plucked her from the sky.

Milo moved aside as the Evissas lifted the newborn up. We all waited. I don't know what I expected to occur next. I think I expected the Evissas to close in a crush around the newborn. But if this was a crush it was the gentlest I had ever seen.

Words came then, softly spoken from the Protector in a language I did not know, and I realized that he must be trying to soothe the newborn, to stop her struggling. But the words only seemed to infuriate the newborn more and her teeth and arm-growths slashed and ripped at the Evissas, until I heard the Protector himself wail with agony. Even so he continued to close his hand gently around the newborn, and though she tore at him, the Protector did not retaliate, merely closed on her gently until he had the newborn entirely sealed in the Evissas.

There was a final frenzy of activity from inside, then silence.

For over a minute nothing happened. Complete silence over Coldharbour. The winds died down. Milo turned and turned in the sky, searching for other enemies. All around us children stopped running and stared upward.

Then, slowly, cautiously, with the greatest care, each of the separate digits of the Evissas de-clenched. One Evissa unfolded and we saw nothing; a second, and we still couldn't see the newborn. A third, and something splashed in a downpour from the sky. And, noticing the brown slick liquid, the blood, the Protector shrieked. It was a shriek of anguish. At the same time he gingerly unfolded the remaining Evissas, until we could see the body of the newborn.

It was a broken body, smashed. And seeing it I suppose we should have wanted to shout with triumph, or at least relief, but we didn't, because the Protector was clearly filled with sorrow. For a moment he held the newborn as if he could not quite believe her body had been so delicate, what he had done.

Then the Protector murmured, 'There is still hope,' whether to us or to the air I don't know, and suddenly the Evissas were racing with the crushed newborn back to the water. That was the first time we saw the Protector's face rise up from the ocean. His blind eye rose out of the water, and under it there was more silver, rising and rising, until at last what I realized must be a mouth, a parting of the mountain-head.

The Protector fastened this parting onto the slack jaw of the newborn. He made a seal and we saw the newborn's body inflate. For several minutes the Protector pumped in his breath, waited for life, pumped in his breath, waited for life, and next to me for some reason the twins were crying. All around me children were crying.

Finally the Protector dropped his lips from the newborn. He held up his Evissas, twisting them in the sky, as if they had betrayed him. He kissed the body of the newborn once, twice, then drew her down with him back into the ocean. The sea was stained with blood, miles of blood. 'Oh, what have I done?' the Protector murmured, as if he was seeking an explanation, or our forgiveness, or both. 'What shame is this?'

The surface of the water shuddered several times, and then the Protector withdrew even his eye from us.

Thirteen
humiliation
THE ROAR

The Roar hurtled towards the Earth.

In she came, unhinged with rage, poisons bursting from her skin, calling out to Carnac to ready him for battle. She gazed at the bright patch of Milo below, and brought forward her clench-limbs. She oiled her flanks and flourished her thread-rapiers in preparation for the orifices of his silver face. She had not considered how she would kill Milo in cold fury before, but she did now. She would devour his head. She would cut off his silver wings. She would take his life ritually, a blood-assassination in the old style, and then she would take each of the other children and kill them as slowly as it was possible to kill anything.

Her last remaining newborn scuttled nervously across her back.

'Why?' the Roar demanded. 'Why did you not help your sister?'

The newborn cowered. It searched for places to hide on her body, clinging to her flanks to avoid the accusation of her eyes. Wherever it went, she made it feel the nip of her poisons.

'Was it for such lack of courage I nourished you all those centuries?' the Roar screamed. 'Did I consume the others that you might live and do this! I lavished attention on you, knowing you needed it more than your sister. Is that why she went alone – to prove herself, because I had not praised her enough?'

The Roar let the final newborn burn in the humiliation of her words.

But her own humiliation was just as great.

To have lost a newborn! She should have suspected one of them would attack while her sifts were still in the oceans, and she could do nothing to stop them until they were retracted. She should have known that her first newborn would go alone, even if the other's nerve failed.

'What happened?' the Roar asked. 'Did you agree to go with your sister, and then falter at the last moment? Perhaps you even encouraged her. Yes, that would be like you, excitable, eager to prove yourself, but too frightened to leave my body.'

Tucked into her mother's thick hair, the last newborn tried not to listen.

'I will make an assassin of you yet,' the Roar thought furiously. 'I will bring you to breeding age, and make you one, whether you are ready or not.'

Her whole body was directly above the Earth now. She wanted to descend on the planet in all her armed glory, but she hesitated. This is exactly how the Protector would wish her to arrive, she realized. Enraged. Furious. Coaxed into hasty decisions. Revealing all her weapons in the first assault.

'Not so exhausted as you led me to believe after all, old

foe,' the Roar mused. 'Concealing so deftly the remaining strength of your Evissas. But I suppose you had nothing to do except plan for this in your ocean-prison, did you? Nothing to do except plan and wait. You are older and more mature than our first battle, when you spread your body before me with such fear.'

The Roar considered her attacking options. An all-out strike, revealing the totality of her weapons, was out of the question. A smaller target first, something to test the level of resistance. No doubt the Protector would be expecting an attack against the silver child, so why not begin by slaying one of the lesser children? Like for like. Her newborn's life for one of the loved ones. Fitting enough. Walter, for example. Simply threaten any of the others, the Roar thought, and he rushes to the source of danger. Or perhaps the twins, too frail to run. Or Thomas.

Or Jenny. The weapon itself. The real danger. Her control over the animals was increasingly a threat.

But Jenny could not truly threaten without Helen.

Helen, the Roar thought, is the key. She provides the information Jenny needs. Kill Helen and Jenny could not become a weapon. Indeed, until Helen was dead there was always the risk she might find a weakness for Jenny to exploit. Her mental powers were developing at extraordinary speed, unlike anything the Roar had seen in any species before.

Kill her fast, she thought. But how? How to expose her? Perhaps via the male, the father, the one outside the Barrier. Yes, it might work. He was further from the Evissas than the others. The Roar doubted the Protector would be able to shield him from a determined attack. And Helen would not easily recover from his death.

Or – and this intrigued the Roar even more – was there a

way she could use Helen's power to destroy the Protector? The Protector made the children feel cherished and secure. Could she find a way to puncture that – to make Helen, at least, suspicious of it. To make her doubt the Protector. If a direct attack failed, why not try persuasion?

Many possibilities, then.

The Protector could not anticipate them all.

While the Roar decided her strategy, she tested out each of her weapons. Now that the food in the southern oceans had renewed her strength, more of those weapons were available to her. A small penetrating dart would work best against Milo, she realized. A thread-rapier – if she could get sufficiently close.

But the Protector would expect that. What form of attack would the Protector be least likely to anticipate? Better still, could she find a way to test the silver child and hurt the Protector at the same time?

The Roar allowed her assassin-training and battle experience to flood back to her, going over the threats and opportunities as she had done so often before, in the days when her assassin-team might enjoy taking a century to plan a kill.

Of course, there was no such time to plan this kill. The children below were evolving at a remarkable pace.

Casting her mind back, the Roar recalled her own mother's battles, and those of her mother before that. Once, while all three females were still alive, they had represented the ultimate perfection of the Roar fighting-combination: an assassin-team of six in all, three females and three males: the faster two males to catch the Protector, the third male, fastest of all, held in reserve should the Protector escape in a final spurt. The heavier females cruising in to finish the task: two clamping and holding down the dangerous Evissas, the last female landing on the Protector's neck and performing the execution. Each female taking the turn of executioner over the span of centuries.

'Are you listening?' the Roar demanded scornfully of her final newborn. 'Are you listening to the achievements of your ancestors?'

The newborn cowered behind her neck, but was also eager to know what was ahead. Battle! She wanted to jump onto her mother's face and see ahead, but was still afraid of her poisons.

'Go to my stomach,' the Roar said. 'Do not move from there.'

Once the newborn was safely inside her, the Roar stared at the planet below. She chose her target. Then she picked a combination of weapons.

Her attack was bound to surprise Milo. If she carried out the attack perfectly it would also surprise the Protector. No matter how long it had pondered in its ocean confinement, she doubted it would anticipate this particular blend of tactics.

Roaring one final time to shake off any last fears she called out to Carnac, telling him to be ready for her call. And Carnac answered. Trustworthy and impatient, he ached for combat. He could not wait to devastate the Unearthers.

The Roar scoured the moon to sharpen her teeth.

She oiled her jaws. She readied some, not all, of her weapons.

To cast as much fear into the minds of the children as possible she approached from the direction of the sun and enveloped the Earth in her black umbra.

Fourteen

bulk

HELEN

There was no warning. One moment the sun shone over the entire northern hemisphere; the next darkness fell. No more feeding, I realized. No more delays. No more exploratory breaths or newborn raids.

The Roar was ready.

Milo reacted immediately, brightening to compensate for the missing sun. Pulling on my jacket, I stumbled out of the shack. All across Coldharbour, children were looking for relatives and friends or finding shelter.

Milo flew high into the sky, cupping the air with huge sweeps. Going into his mind, I found him desperately reviewing every battle option the Protector had taught him. But he was confused. Nothing had prepared Milo for whatever specific attack this was.

He took up a steep, angled position in the sky. His torso was inclined like a javelin, his inner wings bent backward like a hawk's. I understood why: this body angle offered maximum manoeuvrability. From it he could resist a strike from most directions. But there was another reason: it meant presenting less of his *own* body for the Roar to damage, less of a target. It was vital that he protect himself. He knew that the Roar's best chance to kill him was now, before he discovered the nature of her attack.

The change in Milo's position left much of Coldharbour exposed. Children who had always been under the safety of his wings felt naked and rushed for cover. Walter's visitors crowded around the shack, urging me towards the closest underground tunnel.

'No,' I said, realizing that if I was to be any use to Milo I needed to be able to see what was happening.

Dark clouds scudded across the sky. They briefly covered Milo's face, then he was free of them again. Without the warmth of the sun, the wind was intensely cold. Children huddled together, shivering from it.

'TAKE SHELTER,' Milo called down. 'THE ROAR IS COMING. TAKE SHELTER. I WILL SHIELD YOU AND SO WILL THE PROTECTOR. CHILDREN ON YOUR OWN JOIN THE CHILD-FAMILIES. PARENTS NOT CLOSE TO THE BARRIER MAKE YOUR WAY UNDER MY WINGS, SO THAT I MAY SAFEGUARD YOU. OLDER – '

Suddenly Milo broke off. His eyes snapped upwards. He rose higher into the sky, his face tilting towards something beyond.

And the Roar came for him.

She dropped her bulk downward towards the Earth.

We saw nothing at first, but we could *feel* that bulk – a rise in air pressure, our ears popping as she lowered her vastness through the atmosphere.

'Walter!' shrieked despondent children all around me.

But he wasn't coming. He was stuck in western Coldharbour. There was no way Walter could make it back in time. Jenny, being thrown violently from side to side in the pouch as he ran, was trying to rouse the animals. Thomas's beauty flowed into her, and as it did so throughout Coldharbour dogs yelped as if they were on fire. They could smell the Roar. To their sensitive muzzles she stank of bile and the debris of space.

The Protector cut into my thoughts.

'Helen! Remember! Do not dwell on the living or the dead, but on what can be *done*! While the Roar attacks, a chance will arise to search again for weaknesses.'

'When should I look for them?'

'When the situation is most grave.'

'How will I know when – '

'You will know.'

'How – '

'*You will know!*'

The Protector hastily withdrew from my mind. I felt him gathering himself for what was ahead.

And then something bigger than Milo entered the clouds. I saw matted hair, and a bulging underbelly.

But that was only a fraction of the Roar. Somewhere, out of sight, there was also a head. And from that direction came an appendage. Whatever it was, the Roar extended it towards Milo so rapidly that he did not have time to raise his wings in self-defence. The appendage was massive and crude. The two digits on the end were more like armoured grapplers than fingers, and though the Roar had allowed me to discover next to nothing about her weapons I knew this one.

A clench-limb.

The first of them seized Milo's neck. The second clamped

the top of his skull, preventing his head from turning. With all his strength Milo tried to break away, but there was no breaking from this mastery of grip. That was the purpose of the clench-limbs: to hold an enemy in place until the right weapon could be deployed to kill it.

Slowly, Milo's head was dragged up. Once his face was pointed at the Roar's matted underbelly the hair parted, and two barbs came sweeping down. Both were thin, glinting, flexible, whip-like.

Each ended in a spiked tip.

As soon Milo saw the tips he shuddered, fighting to twist his head away even more strenuously. But the clench-limbs held him. They held him and the barbed tips swung towards his nose. What were these barbs? For some reason they sought out Milo's nostrils. They prodded and probed, dangling lower, seeking the openings.

Then, from across the ocean, a set of Evissas rose out of the waves. I couldn't believe the swiftness with which they came.

The Roar, however, was ready for them.

The barbed spikes were withdrawn, and in their place a third clench-limb shot down.

It met the Evissas halfway up the sky.

The impact was incredible. The sound of so much weight and fury coming together burst like a shock wave across Coldharbour. Almost equal in strength, the clench-limb and the Evissas grappled one another, each seeking the advantage, the better grip. Meanwhile, the Roar's other clench-limbs continued to squeeze Milo. The one around his neck had the tightest hold.

Seeing that Milo could not breathe, the Protector thrust his Evissas into the space above the clouds. The Roar shuddered repeatedly from whatever the Evissas did there, but her clench-limbs remained in place around Milo. She did not relax her grip. If anything the clench-limb around his throat tightened.

'Come to me!' the Protector cried, but Milo could not. So the Protector had no choice. He had no choice except to raise his whole head out of the ocean to reach Milo. He did so, preparing to offer Milo his own breath, and it was then I realized the Roar's true purpose.

Milo had not been her primary target after all.

All of this had been to expose the Protector.

For suddenly several more of the stabbing barbs descended in long rows, and this time they ignored Milo. Instead, they entered the sensitive, still damaged, areas surrounding the Protector's eye.

The Protector wailed and withdrew in pain – a pain so intense it made me jump.

I rebounded from it – and rushed into the mind of the Roar. I sought a weakness, any weakness. But the Roar was prepared for me: she shut her mind.

Milo tried again to breathe. He could not.

I think the knowledge of that must have driven the Protector to act, even if he failed. From the ocean, from whatever terrible injury he had suffered, he flung out his Evissas again. They fumbled for the clench-limb holding Milo's neck. They found it, reached behind – and stabbed. The clench-limb flinched open. It was back moments later, feeling for the neck again but not before Milo, in a last spasm, tore his head loose.

He broke away.

And dropped like a great angel from the sky.

Gasping, wings folded across his chest, he fell.

Then, beating wildly, he just managed to keep himself aloft.

Under him children tried to get to cover, but of course had Milo fallen they would have been crushed.

The Protector's Evissas retracted like lifeless objects and sank beneath the waves.

I went to the Roar's mind, but was again shut out.

Above us, Milo filled his lungs. Glowing feebly, he spread his wings. They were undamaged. He flexed them once, twice, three times. He brightened again. Hovering, he tried to clear his thoughts.

Before he could do so the Roar changed her point of attack. She was no longer so interested in Milo or the Protector. She swung her belly over Coldharbour, away from them.

Towards the west.

Thomas, I thought.

I didn't know if it was Thomas the Roar had suddenly made her target. It could have been Walter or the twins. It was probably Jenny.

Then I realized it was all of them.

The hairy stomach of the Roar opened and excreted a wetness. The wetness flowed like oil. It slid down the hair, moistening it, dribbling down the length of six or seven individual hair strands. It gathered there, beading on the ends.

Drips. Blue drips. Even in the silver-stained sky the drips were a stunning blue.

Poison. It had to be. What else could look so beautiful?

In the ocean, I sensed the wounded Protector trying to help, but unable to.

From western Coldharbour, the distant Jenny desperately pulled in her arms to bring the birds towards her. Flocks which had been useless against the huge clench-limbs of the Roar instantly turned and flew westward.

The poison gathered on the Roar's hair ends. Each drip was a blue so clear that you could see through it to the abdomen beyond. That abdomen now shivered violently to help the poisons disperse. Then the Roar swept the hairs upwards in a long, almost graceful curve, dispersing the drips across the whole of western Coldharbour.

Milo tried to prevent the poison reaching the ground. One of his wings swung out as a shield towards the children, but it could not reach western Coldharbour in time. Only those birds stationed over the area were in position to stop the poison. Flock after flock spread their wings.

And the poison fell on them like great killing drops of rain.

I don't know how many birds the poison touched. It seemed to me that the whole of Coldharbour was filled with wings. They died flapping those wings. As the poison fell the birds spread their feathers and sacrificed their lives. They aligned themselves in multiple layers, so there would be no gaps through which the poison might penetrate their wing shield, and then each took a tiny amount of poison, falling instantly dead from the skies.

To be replaced by more, falling, more, falling, more, falling.

Finally the poisons were spent. I peered up at the belly of the Roar, expecting new spurts to emerge. And for a moment the belly did ease open again, and I saw the deadly blue line the opening. But then the Roar seemed to change her mind. Either that or she did not have enough poison to continue.

I had so little insight into her mind that I didn't know which.

My ears popped again as the Roar raised her body.

But this time Milo was ready.

The Roar pulled her clench-limbs to safety, but as she withdrew her abdomen Milo brought a wing across the sky. It was an exact arc of movement, precision-timed, and with the leading edge positioned like a scalpel he sliced part of the abdomen off.

The shriek of pain from the Roar was unlike anything inflicted by the Protector.

For a while the Roar stayed where she was, still up there, one of her eyes penetrating the clouds and studying perhaps me, perhaps Milo, perhaps Jenny – as if deciding whether or not to carry on with the attack.

Then she removed the damaged abdomen, and heaved her body beyond the clouds.

But Milo flew after her. He flew after her, and he was faster. His wings took him out of our sight, and before the Roar could reach the sanctuary of space he slashed a bulging area above her abdomen twice. He did it accurately, armed with the Protector's knowledge, and based on weeks of rehearsals in his mind, in case this slight chance should present itself.

The slashes cut into the Roar's digestive tract.

The tract imploded, pumping digestive juices and the active furnaces of two of her stomachs into the body of the Roar.

The second newborn, scuttling from the area, barely escaped with her life.

The Roar screamed over and over as her own juices and stomachs burned her, desperately drawing water from her bowels to quench the fires.

I thought I would be able to enter the Roar's mind at that moment. Surely, now, I would be able to find a way in! But I was wrong. Even with the fires damaging the Roar's body and blurring her judgement, even then, I wasn't able to get inside. The Roar could experience this much pain, and still offer me nothing.

The only thing I discovered was that the injury to her digestive system appalled her. And then the Roar pulled her entire body up and beyond any region where Milo could do her further harm.

The sun returned. As it lit Coldharbour again with mellow warmth, children emerged shivering and bent from their shelters. In our area there were no major injuries – only fractured bones and cuts where people had fallen over or shelters had blown down – but in western Coldharbour dead birds littered the ground. Their stiffening feathers were streaked with blue. The blue was so vibrant that some youngsters had to be stopped from touching them. The remaining flocks of birds circled overhead, mourning their companions. They flew aimlessly. Without further guidance from Jenny they weren't sure whether to search for Milo or stay aloft and wait for the Roar.

After a time, Milo reappeared in the upper sky.

One of his wings was slightly damaged. He raised and lowered it tentatively. There were also deep purple bruises on his neck and his temple. If he had still possessed hands, I think he would have probed his neck, to test how it felt. Instead, he took up his old position over Coldharbour, parallel to the horizon, his wings once again stretched over us. Both his silver eyes pointed downwards. I knew why: he was counting – counting the number of children in the west.

People across Coldharbour expected Milo to speak. They wanted him to. They wanted to hear that the Roar was dead, or so badly injured that she might as well be. Above all, the children wanted news about the Protector. And Milo wanted nothing more than to give them hope, but he didn't want to lie. He knew that the Roar was still far from defeated, and the Protector terribly injured. So in the end he stayed silent, encouraging the remaining birds to the clefts of his wings and enfolding them there.

With no information forthcoming from Milo, everyone's attention in our area fell on me.

One of Walter's visitors wiped her sleeve across her face. 'Is the Protector alive?' she demanded. 'Is he?'

'I don't know,' I said.

I reached out for him, but felt nothing. Was he too frail even to contact me? I waited for dappled sunlight. When it didn't come I resigned myself to wait longer. For over an hour I sat with the other children of Coldharbour, gazing out to sea, still stunned by the severity of the Roar's attack. I hoped to spot – I don't know, something; an Evissa, perhaps an eye; anything to indicate that the Protector might still be alive.

I waited for his voice.

And heard, instead, another's. *Her* voice.

The Roar.

I'd been so distracted that I'd allowed her into my mind.

I tried to pull away immediately, but was unable to. Not this time. I felt sure she'd attack me, but no, this was not an attack. The opposite, in fact. A welcome. She welcomed me. An invitation to listen.

I tried not to. The last time it had nearly led to Jenny's death.

'You are mistaken about my intentions,' said the Roar.

Her voice was warm and engaging.

I didn't allow her any deeper. I could protect myself a little by keeping her at the edge of my mind. This time I wouldn't fall for any of her traps.

'No,' the Roar said. 'This is no trap. I am a killer. I admit that. I am a killer and an assassin. I am both those things, but I am not the worst. The one you call the Protector is your true enemy. I have killed, but only ever for food. It is your beloved Protector who kills for pleasure.'

I pretended to listen to the Roar, while secretly probing again for weaknesses Jenny could use.

There was no response from the Protector. Could he hear this?

'He?' the Roar mocked. '*He.* The Protector has no sex, Helen, not as you understand it. It is not male or female, except what it can convince you to believe – what you wish it to be. It has lived with your species since the dawn of your history. In that time it has learned how to gain your trust. More than that: how to make you *adore* it. For each of you adores it, don't you? It wants that. Why do you think it created the Barrier? Not to protect you, but to isolate children from their parents. The Protector wanted to make sure you would all look for guidance only to it. And, in your case, Helen, the Protector had an additional problem: your real father was already inside Coldharbour. He had to be removed. He was far too much of an influence. And how well the Protector has substituted for your father! Once your first thoughts always went to him, didn't they? Not any more! It is the Protector you think of first now!'

I tried to ignore that, but I couldn't.

There was still no response from the Protector.

'That is why the Protector delayed so long before it spoke to you, Helen. It could have spoken earlier, but it wanted to know everything about you first. The Protector knew how important you were to its plans. It wanted to be sure. It wanted its first words to bind you to it and break your heart.'

I thought about Dad. It had been a while since I thought of him – but surely not for the reason the Roar suggested.

'Do you remember how painful it was for Milo to become the silver child?' the Roar asked. 'Do you think it had to be so brutal? No, it did not. But the Protector wanted his shield over him quickly, so he helped Milo to evolve. And do you think your precious Protector really cared for the twins? Cared that Emily nearly drowned? The Protector knew *you* cared, that is all. It brought them down and made them love it to impress you, Helen. Because it needed you. Oh, the Protector needed you most of all. It wanted you to fashion Jenny into the weapon of its choice. That way it would not need to risk itself in battle with me at all.'

The Roar opened up a pathway through her mind, and I felt myself drawn into it. Inside I saw the silver bodies of the Protectors surrounding the Roar's home world. I saw the Roar, our Roar, trying to get back to her own planet – and prevented from doing so.

'What new lie is this?' I demanded.

'This is us, starving,' came the answer. 'The Protectors tried to starve our species to death. This is why we formed the assassin-teams. It was a necessity. But even that did not work, for the Protectors then went after our young. They aimed to exterminate our species by killing our youngest.'

I half shut my mind, continuing to search for weaknesses.

'They are *species* killers, Helen,' the Roar went on. 'They wait on the food worlds in the outlying regions, just as yours waited for me. They know there is nowhere else for us to go. They wait for us there, and they are fanatical. A Protector would rather die than give a meal to any Roar. It would rather die than allow a newborn to live.'

'Liar!' I thought. 'I saw how he tried to save your newborn!'

'No. You saw a clenched hand and mistook it for a caress.

Those Evissas closed with the perfect poise of the assassin on my child. The Protector merely made it seem an accident to you. It knows your species, Helen. It knows what brings you to tears. It knows what *moves* you.'

'That isn't true. It isn't.'

'I guarantee you this,' the Roar said. 'Once it kills the final newborn, the Protector will find a way to kill you all as well. That is the way of its species. They kill anything that is a threat.'

I tried to shut my mind, but couldn't.

'You are the killer here,' I thought.

The Roar said, 'You owe me nothing. I have no reason to expect your mercy, nor do I ask it. But save the last of my newborn. Do not allow the Protector to kill her, as it will, though no doubt it will conceal that from you as effectively as it has concealed everything else. Until, that is, it is ready to kill you as well.'

I couldn't pull away from the Roar.

'Hasn't the Protector always been uncommonly interested in the fate of the newborn?' the Roar asked, holding me in. 'Haven't you ever thought to question that? The Protector longs to deny life to my species. It wants the newborn dead.'

None of this was true. It couldn't be.

'Do you truly accept,' the Roar asked, 'that Evissas barely able to rise out of the water could afterwards grapple me with such conviction? Do you? When the Protector girded its silver loins, you must have sensed the strength still left. How could you not feel that?'

'I do not believe you!' I screamed out loud.

But did I? Either the Roar's words were true – or, I realized with horror, she's using me.

How could she be using me?

With a huge effort, I managed to pull away from the

mental clutch of the Roar. There followed a scream of frustration from her.

I shakily stood up – and went into Jenny's mind.

She was still in western Coldharbour. Her chin was raised, her eyes locked wide, waiting for a final confirmation from me. Thomas lay next to her. Beauty poured through him, enough to give Jenny whatever she needed, enough for any purpose I could imagine.

Jenny was no longer quite human. She was half-human. Half-human and half-weapon.

A new weapon. Not one to attack the Roar this time.

The perfect weapon, instead, to attack the Protector.

Jenny's body had transformed. It was the same shape now as the holes the Roar had stabbed around the Protector's eye. Those wounds went deep, but the weapon Jenny had become could go deeper. Her head bulged, glistening with the edges that would cut through the flesh of the Protector.

I knew at once that Jenny's new shape was a more effective weapon than any the Roar had. She could kill the Protector easily.

In fact, there was more than one way she could kill him. I knew enough now, given the Protector's injuries, to kill him in several ways.

If I'd believed a little more, I realized, if I'd stayed just a while longer inside the Roar's mind, I might have been completely convinced.

'Oh, so that is what you are doing,' I thought. 'Oh, I nearly believed you. I nearly did.'

Jenny gasped as my mind emptied of purpose. She slumped to her knees. Thomas held his beauty back from her again, though he could hardly bear to. He lay there, his head pillowed in Walter's hands.

For a moment I stood in the soil outside the shack,

terrified by the power that existed between the three of us. And then I felt the relief of the Protector, as he managed to make the faintest contact with my mind again. 'Helen,' he murmured. 'Helen.'

'I believed her,' I wept. 'I'm sorry! I did! For a second I did! While I was in there with her, I believed her. And I still haven't found her true weakness. I found nothing!'

'The blame is mine,' the Protector said, his voice so quiet I barely registered it. 'I should have warned you more about her ... what she can do ... many centuries I listened to her words, and my mind was nearly lost also.'

'What are we going to do?' I thought.

I couldn't hear what the Protector said next. To help me understand he formed a picture in my mind. A face.

Thomas's.

the hazel-eyed girl

THOMAS

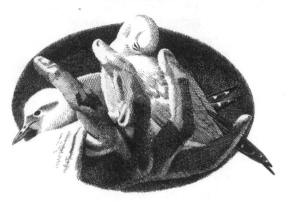

Throughout the transformation from deadly weapon back to child not even Walter could comfort Jenny. It took several minutes for her grossly swollen skull to return to normal, and afterwards she was inconsolable. She hid inside the pouch and refused to talk.

'If you were any paler,' Emily whispered, trying to coax her out, 'you'd give me a fright.'

'Any paler,' Freda added, 'and you'd be Snow White.'

Jenny just crept deeper within and closed her eyes.

At least inside the pouch she didn't have to see the birds. A few – those only grazed by the poisons – were still alive as we walked across western Coldharbour. Tearing off a shirt-sleeve, Walter picked them up, and some birds actually jiggled about in his hands for a while, but every last one was dead before we got halfway back to the shack.

'Help me d-do this, Tommy,' he murmured when the last

one stopped moving, and I scooped out a pile of earth for him to place the birds inside.

It was a terrible return journey. We were ankle-deep in dead birds until we left western Coldharbour, and I couldn't stop thinking about the Protector.

'You can't know what's happened to 'im!' Freda hissed, when I tried to talk about it. 'Only Helen will know for sure! Ee ain't dead. We'd feel it ...'

'What if ee's dying, though, Free?' Emily whispered.

As soon as she said that I thought the twins were bound to go straight down to whatever was left of the Protector under the waves, but they didn't. Instead, Emily choked back her emotions and straightened out her dress. 'Stop,' she said firmly to Walter.

'We need to get back to the s-shack,' he protested. 'We – '

'No!' She cut him off. 'We're staying put! Toms never found his special child there anyways. We'll find it now. If there is one,' she added under her breath.

She slipped to the right of me, while Freda sidled round to my left. Both girls walked in a slow circle, testing the air with their noses.

'Time to find someone,' Freda said, rubbing my shins encouragingly. 'Like old times. What yer waiting for? Find uz a pearl.'

'Is it a boy,' Emily said, 'or is it a girl?'

I gazed around. There were more children than ever following us. From my perch on Walter's shoulder, I could even see those on the outskirts of Coldharbour drifting our way.

Surely my beauty couldn't be for them all?

Freda stroked my arm. 'C'mon,' she urged me. 'It's you they're placing their 'ope in, Toms. It always was, if yer beauty 'ad been ready. Me and Emms knew that first day we met we couldn't keep you all to ourselves.'

There was a teenage girl near us. Only a few feet away. She held up her hand as if she knew me, though I'd never seen her before.

Should I touch her?

It seemed to take a long time for her hand to reach mine, or mine to reach hers. Afterwards I could never be sure who had made the first move. One of us – both perhaps – leaned forward. Then, for a moment, I hesitated, remembering Tanni and the Unearthers, what had happened the last time a stranger reached out so earnestly for my beauty. I peered uncertainly at the girl, and she hung back. She didn't grasp at me the way the Unearthers had.

But was it safe to touch her? How could I be sure?

'Don't you trust your beauty?' Freda asked.

A good question. No. I didn't. Not completely. It had flowed freely into the Unearthers. It had flowed freely into Jenny when she was becoming the wrong weapon.

'I trust you, Freda,' I said. 'Is this girl the one? I don't want any more mistakes.'

'She thinks she is.'

'But what do *you* think?'

The girl was virtually next to me now. Her fingers trembled slightly in the breeze.

No one around us moved.

I didn't get any closer to the girl. I wanted to, but I was afraid.

The twins wavered, unsure what advice to offer. Their glances roved anxiously between me and Walter. They'd always known what child needed my beauty in the past, but this time I could tell they had no idea whether I should approach the girl or run.

I turned to face her again.

What harm, after all, could it do to touch her? She

seemed ordinary enough: not tall, not short, the same Coldharbour muck clinging to her clothes as the rest of us. Eleven or twelve years old, with hazel-brown eyes. Nothing special about those eyes. The most common coloured eyes in the world. I wondered how long she'd been following me. All morning? Longer?

Her body shook slightly. She was still waiting – for what? My permission to approach? She moved to within easy grabbing distance of me. A trace of burning rubbish from the tower fires wafted over us.

'Touch me,' she whispered.

I swallowed. Walter stood there, ready to snatch me away if there was any danger. A strand of the girl's long dark hair blew into my face, and as she stepped forward I nearly put all my fingers out at once. I nearly put my whole hand against her neck. At the last second I panicked and it was only the skin of my index finger that grazed her lips.

The girl was not shy. She was not shy to demand more of my touch. She eased my hand around and rubbed the back of my palm gently against her cheek.

In that instant, I knew what I expected to feel. A jolt of recognition. A rush of beauty. Passion.

Instead I felt – nothing.

The girl rubbed my fingers harder. She was shocked, but I tried not to be. This had happened before. When I'd touched Jenny the first time, I'd also felt nothing.

But on that occasion hadn't my beauty been desperate to reach Jenny?

It showed no interest whatsoever in this girl.

Another child – a boy this time, about eight years old – pressed my forearm, and the result was the same.

I looked down at my chest, as if I might question the beauty there. What was wrong? Now, more than ever, I knew how much beauty I had inside. Enough for the girl. Enough for the girl *and* this boy. Enough for any group of children.

'What do you need?' I asked her.

She didn't know.

I turned to Jenny. Climbing out of the pouch, she sat on her heels in the mud. She wanted my beauty as much as the others. I felt the desire for it rise like heat through her body, saw her eyes dilate. Saw the whites.

'Help me,' she said.

'What do you need?'

'More of your beauty. More of it. We all do. More.'

'Take it, then. What are you waiting for?' I shuffled another step towards her. I knelt beside her.

'I can't,' she said.

'Why?'

'There's something … missing.'

She was right. Somehow I still wasn't ready.

All this intensity of beauty, and no way to focus or release it!

'Is there no defender here?' I found myself shouting in exasperation. 'There must be! There must be someone! Here! See this?' I rolled up my sleeves to expose the flesh. 'Come on! Anyone! Just touch me!'

So they did. The hazel-eyed girl stepped aside, and others took her place. I tapped one girl, then another, then a boy, then several at once. Still nothing happened. Oh, but I could tell they wanted it to! I was surrounded by beauty-hunger! Every child craved this contact with me. Whole child-families were offering themselves. Two older boys gazed at me as if I'd just stirred their souls.

'Walts?' Freda murmured.

I knew why she appealed to him at that moment. He was a defender. If anyone could find other defenders amongst these children, surely it would be Walter. Being taller than anyone else he could see clear across Coldharbour, and he took his time, gazing in all directions. For a while he concentrated on Coldharbour's beaches. Ships were still docking there, and he studied some Japanese children disembarking, swimming through the shallows, dashing up the sands.

'It's all right, Walts,' Emily said gently at last, squeezing his hand. 'It ain't your fault.' She glanced meaningfully at Freda. 'You thinking the same thing, Free? Your nose going crazy on yer, too?'

'Mm,' Freda said, giving the air a last sniff. 'There ain't one child. We'd 'ave rooted 'em out by now.'

'Exactly!' Emily agreed. 'There're so many I dunno where to turn! That's why we can't find your child, Toms,' she said huskily. 'Because it ain't one child at all.' She swept her arms to indicate all of Coldharbour. 'It's this one' – she held up the arm of the hazel-eyed girl – 'and this one' – the boy. 'It's not one, Toms. It ain't just Milo or Jenny any more. Don't yer see how much yer beauty's grown? *It's all of 'em.*'

'All of them?'

'Get uz back north, Walts!' Freda said, scrambling onto his arm. 'Get uz back to Helen!'

Walter ran all the way. Helen, hands on hips, was waiting for us outside the shack.

'No,' she said before Walter had even put us down, her eyes red with tears. 'I don't know how to release the beauty. I don't! I've ... tried! I should know, but I don't. The answer's tied in with the Roar, somehow, but I can't break through her mind. I can't ...'

She trailed off and the twins pulled her close, but Helen separated herself again and averted her eyes. I think she knew that what she had to tell us next would be too much, at least for Emily.

'Don't you dare say the Protector's dead!' Emily screamed when Helen cradled her face. 'Ee ain't dead! Oh, ee can't be!'

Helen waited for her to calm down. Then she said, 'He might be. I've stopped hearing him. But even if he's alive I think he's too injured to help any more. We're on our own. It's up to us now. There, I've said it.'

'We've got M-Milo,' Walter said.

'Yes,' Helen answered. 'Milo can still fly, and the animals and birds will stay with us, but without the Protector ...'

Walter excused himself, anxious to be shoring up the defences around the shack. The twins joined him outside.

So did Jenny, my beauty drifting towards her as she left.

'It's for the animals,' Helen explained. 'There are no limits to Jenny's range now. She's reaching out to the whole world, bringing the last of them to us.'

I nodded. 'But they won't be able to stop the Roar on their own, will they? That's what you're thinking.'

'No. They won't.'

'You used to think Milo and the animals might be enough.'

'I was wrong about that, Thomas.'

'Is there any way Milo can save us?'

'If there is, he'll find it.'

'But you don't think he will.'

'No.'

I stared hard at her, wanting a different answer.

'Do you want me to pretend?' Helen said angrily. 'Is that what you want me to do? Tell you it's going to be OK? Of all people, Thomas, do you want me to lie about our chances?'

'No ... of course not. I'm sorry,' I said, lowering my gaze. I walked a few steps around the shack, then looked up at her again. My mouth felt dry. 'If the Roar gets to us, what ...

will it be like? Will it be quick? Will *we* be the first to die?' I
don't know what made me ask that, but suddenly it seemed
important.

'I doubt it,' Helen replied darkly. 'In fact, no, I don't
think it'll be quick at all. She doesn't want us dying quickly.
And she's still got a promise to keep to her final newborn.
About me in particular. She'll keep me alive as long as she
can. I'll be the *very* last.'

I nodded, not knowing what to say.

'I'm not giving up,' Helen said. 'I'm not giving up any
more than you are. The final attack won't be long now. If
Milo can ... I don't know ... injure the Roar somehow, she
could still be vulnerable. I might still be able to get inside her
mind.'

'When will she attack again?'

'Whenever she's ready.'

'At least she won't be able to surprise Milo,' I said, grasp-
ing for a shred of hope. 'Not like the first time she attacked.
He'll be better prepared.'

Helen shook her head. 'No, Thomas, not really. Milo has-
n't even seen the worst of the Roar's weapons yet. The first
attack was a test of his strength. The next will be different,
overwhelming. And remember: it's not just the Roar Milo
has to worry about. There's her second newborn as well.'

'And Carnac,' I said.

'Yes. I think that's when we'll know the final battle is starting. When Carnac attacks. That's when the Roar will come
after us. When Carnac makes his move against the
Unearthers.'

sixteen

carnac

TANNI

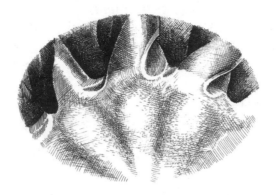

We waited. One-hundred-and-ninety-eight of us Unearthers, cracking up in the freaky tunnel darkness, waiting for a monster.

Two days had passed since we thought Carnac was coming after our metal hides. Since then he'd kind of shuffled around below us six or seven times. Just enough to get our attention. Probably he was only moving his weight around, staying comfy until Mother gave him the call. Or maybe he was doing it to keep us all on edge. I favoured that theory myself.

I'd lost it before. Totally lost it. That first time we thought Carnac was attacking, for a few seconds my nerve went completely. When the rest of the Unearthers saw me mumbling away to myself a minor panic followed, with three pairs making a dash for it back to the surface.

I didn't try to stop them – no point trying to terrorize

anyone into submission – but it was my fault, and I was sure others would follow.

Luckily for me, they returned before anyone else drifted away. Nothing to do with my leadership skills. Of all things, I had the Roar to thank. Her attack sent them scurrying back down. And what a vivid story they told us about that attack! Even down here we'd noticed the Roar making her move. We hadn't seen it, of course, but we'd felt it – a compression in the rocks; a tightening.

We'd immediately assumed the drills-down position, and waited.

And waited. And waited.

While clever old Carnac stayed eerily quiet. Not attacking. Not a sound.

The returning Unearthers, thank goodness, brought some much-needed water in rucksacks on their backs, and as we thirstily unscrewed the tops with our teeth morale actually improved for a while. Most Unearthers began to feel safer *down here*! Ridiculous, but if you had to choose between the Roar and Carnac, it was obvious you wouldn't choose the Roar. I overheard one drill-team leader stressing that to a small boy in her team.

'At least we only have to face Carnac,' she said. 'That's not as bad as the Roar, is it?' She waited until she got a tiny nod. 'Up there, we'll just be a nuisance with these drills, won't we?' Another tiny nod. 'The child-families will have enough to do when the Roar attacks. You don't want them having to worry about us as well, do you?'

The little boy shook his head emphatically. He seemed to be drinking in her words. Then she turned away, and as soon as she did I saw his bottom lip wobbling. He wouldn't have minded one of those big child-families up there taking care of him, after all.

I was especially concerned about the younger Unearthers now that we'd entered a fourth day down here. Our food stocks were almost non-existent. While none of our metal-plated stomachs grumbled quite like the old ones had, we still needed to eat. We'd been on low rations so long that we were all finding it harder to concentrate.

Parminder, I have to say, was brilliant. She somehow kept up everyone's spirits in the nearest drill teams with an almost unending stream of Unearther jokes and breezy chit-chat about the future. Oh yes! Don't think we'd forgotten about the future! Life beyond Carnac! Life after the Roar! Since we were scared stiff, and wanted very much to live, there was plenty of ongoing talk about that! We even half-jokingly, half-seriously, came up with a whole host of problems only our big metal bodies were likely to suffer from. For instance, a tendency to expand in hot weather. For instance, grinding noisy joints. And how about metal fatigue in middle and old age? Oh, and someone suggested we might have a problem with magnets. No dentists, though. That was the good news. With metal teeth, you couldn't get decay. Unless our teeth rusted, of course. We spent half an hour debating that one.

One time, after we'd slowly shared the last dregs of one of our last water bottles, Parminder put her head up to mine and pulled a face.

'I'm glad there're no mirrors down here,' she muttered. 'If I look anything like you, that is.'

'You look just like me,' I told her.

'Hey girls,' Parminder called out loudly. 'Did you hear that? We can't end up looking like the boys, can we? First priority when we get out of here is some decent clothes and some make-up. Girls, we're going to need plenty of make-up!'

Someone near her sniffed. 'We'd still completely stand out.'

'No, we'll be all right,' Parminder said airily. 'A bit of foundation to cover the metal. Well, more than a bit, obviously. But once that's on, it'd be interesting, wouldn't it? I mean, what sort of lipstick goes well with metal? We've got a whole new fashion industry to invent, girls. All sorts of possibilities there. No doubt about it, though, we're definitely going to get some funny looks from those boys when we start dating. Of course, they'll think twice before they say anything nasty to our faces.'

'We'll need jobs,' someone else said. 'I know – lumberjacks! We could become lumberjacks!' And for some reason that made us all laugh.

Then someone whispered, 'I heard something.'

Dead silence fell instantly. We all listened. At first I thought it was just our old pal Carnac making one of his usual small shuffles under us, but no, it was too loud for that. I wanted to call the teams into the drills-down position, but I needed to be sure before scaring the small kids to death all over again.

Then we heard a cracking noise below, followed by a deep intake of breath.

An actual breath. We'd never heard that before – Carnac drawing in air.

I stood up immediately, dragging Parminder with me, and shouted, 'All drill teams get into position. Hands down! Hands – ' But I didn't need to finish. The teams were already doing it. We'd practised so often that it had become second-nature even to the youngsters.

But that breath! How close did it put Carnac? Certainly closer than I'd thought. He'd probably been creeping up all this time. Sly old Carnac. He'd been in our heads once. We knew just how shrewd he was. The nearer he got the more quiet he probably stayed. Lulling us.

But then we heard absolutely nothing. Ten minutes of nothing. I felt sure Carnac was playing with us. Another sliding movement followed, directly below. A stealthy one this time. After that, silence again for over five minutes. Finally I stood the teams down from full to half-alert.

What was old Carnac up to? I had a feeling he'd try to surprise us, regardless of what the Roar did. Most likely he'd co-ordinate his attack with her – and we'd feel the rocks compressing as we'd done before – but we couldn't depend on that. Carnac was a devious fellow. He might attack shortly before the Roar. Or he might not wait at all.

'Do you get the feeling,' Parminder whispered to me, 'that Carnac can't wait to get at us?'

'Yes,' I said. 'I do.'

We stayed in semi-battle readiness, our drills close to the tunnel floor, crouched down, breathing in hot air. For eight more minutes we waited. Except for the teams occasionally checking off with each other, and small encouragements from the leaders and deputies, they were eight minutes of utter silence. Five more minutes followed. Four more.

'Can we stand down?' one team leader asked me.

I considered it.

'Yes, but stay alert.'

The teams half-relaxed again. Some stretched out on the floor. Others slumped against the rocks. A few slept. I'd been surprised at how often the smaller kids fell asleep after a full-alert like this, but it was incredibly tiring for them to stay in that tensed-up downward posture. Sleep was also a little escape from what was happening. We all needed that some-times. But I made sure the leaders staggered the sleep pat-terns, never resting themselves unless their deputy was awake, and never more than half the team sleeping at the same time. No whole-team rests, though it was tempting.

I wasn't having Carnac catch us that way.

A while later, and four pairs of older Unearthers I'd asked to go to the surface for more supplies returned. They'd brought some decent food with them, too: bread, sugar, slices of ham, even biscuits. Parminder had sarcastically put in an order for ice-cream sundae when they left, 'or some lemonade or orange ice-pops, if that's all you can get.' She had to make do with sharing a crust of bread with me and sucking on a sugar lump.

'There's news,' the team leader of the returning team murmured, crouching down beside us.

'Go on.'

'There's no one up on the surface above us, for a start. Not a soul. Totally deserted. They've all gone south and west. They're expecting Carnac to come up right where we are. And there's something else.' He hesitated. 'The Protector ...'

'Keep your voice down,' I warned him.

'OK.' He shuffled forward. 'They're saying the Protector's dead. At least no one's heard him recently.'

I nodded. Like those on the surface, we'd heard the voice of the Protector. I knew many of the Unearthers were placing all their hope in him.

'Will you keep that information to yourself for now?' I asked.

'No problem.' He looked at me. 'There's something else as well. Everyone's scared up there, Tanni. They're terrified. They're more scared than we are.'

Parminder laughed grimly. 'Told you,' she muttered. 'They'll all be coming down here soon.'

I hoped the news about the Protector wouldn't spread too fast, but one of the other returning Unearthers talked about it before I could reach him. So I tried to stress the good news. Milo had fought off the Roar, hadn't he? He'd won the first battle, hadn't he? I also made sure the team leaders dispensed extra food rations, to improve the mood. As I strode around with Parminder, trying to calm the teams down, I had an intense wish to see Thomas again. I suddenly wanted him down here with me. He'd always offered good advice when I needed it. I wondered what his advice would have been now. Hold it together for us up there, I thought.

We veered all that day between anxious attempts to chat/pretend life was going to be OK in some rust-free future and pure fear. Fear won in the end. We knew it wouldn't be long before Carnac attacked. Hours at most, probably less. I let everyone have a double ration of water, and gave the team leaders even more leeway about the food. But the atmosphere deteriorated anyway, and at last, even Parminder was out of jokes – or too nervous to think up any more – and her face sank against my shoulder.

'It's all right,' I murmured.

'No, it's not all right,' she hissed. 'Don't patronize me.'

For several minutes there was almost complete silence between the teams. As if we knew. Then another unbearable few minutes went by.

'Right,' Parminder said loudly. 'I've had it with this! I'm sick to death of just waiting! Let's get it over with. I say we call Carnac up to us.'

'What are you, mad?' someone replied.

'I don't think so,' Parminder said. 'Not a bit of it. Think a minute: if we can goad him up, the Roar won't be ready, will she? He'll attack too soon. That'll help them on the surface. It'll help Milo. Besides, we know Carnac's coming. Why should *he* choose when? Let's get this started. Do any of us really want to wait any more? Come on! Who's with me?'

There was general whispering. Parminder's idea sounded ridiculous, but one boy liked it.

'How are we supposed to get him to come after us, then?' he asked.

'I don't know!' Parminder replied. Then she laughed. 'Shout! Call him names! Oy!' she bellowed at the top of her voice. 'Ugly features, come and get some of this! Did you hear me? I called you ugly!'

'Shush!' someone hissed, but Parminder was just getting started.

'Hey, Carnac! Your mum took a pasting from Milo! Run off to cry, has she? A coward, is she?'

And before I knew what was happening, I could hardly believe it, but loads of us were doing it! Calling Carnac any old name! Swearing and cursing him at the tops of our voices!

'Got to wait for your mum, have you! Little baby! Do what you're told, eh?'

'Hey! Pig-face! Rock-head! I'm talking to you!'

It was crazy, but oh it was such a release! It was such a terrific release! It didn't bring Carnac up to us, but for a while it cut through the fear. We had a brilliant few minutes coming up with the worst insults imaginable.

We couldn't keep it up forever, though. The oppressive silence returned eventually, and talk just petered out again. If anything it was worse than before. Parminder tried to crank up a new round of jokes, but they fell flat. I was just reaching for a swig of water when Carnac made his move.

First we felt the rocks above us compress down. It was that peculiar way we'd noticed before, when the Roar had attacked. Silence followed for about ten seconds. Afterwards, there was a grinding movement from the rocks below. For a moment we were all frozen – then the teams were madly scrabbling to get into position. I hurriedly went through the checks with my own team, and heard the other team leaders doing the same, calling out names, the youngsters piping out their high-pitched responses and getting into the drills-down position.

This time it wasn't a false alarm. The ground below our feet heaved once, then again, hard enough to rock us side-ways. I leaped up and got my team back in position. Then we heard two distinct breaths. I felt them on my face, they were so near. My drill-hand, attached to Parminder's, was shaking. I didn't know if it was me shaking or her. She smiled fiercely at me.

'This is it,' she said – and even though I knew that already, her words sent a ripple of fear through me.

The ground heaved again.

I looked around. All the Unearthers were in position. The leaders had the most nervous team members close by their sides. Some were crying and whimpering, but at least they had their drills correctly pointed down. I suddenly wanted to say something to inspire everyone. But what could I say that wouldn't be trite, that wouldn't make them feel worse than they already did? A few words came into my head, and under any other circumstances they would have been corny, but not here, because it was the only thing in that moment I knew the Unearthers wanted to hear.

'We're going to live through this!' I shouted. 'Do you hear me? Every one of you is going to come out of this alive!'

And then he came at us.

Seventeen

milo

HELEN

'Walts!' Freda squealed.

The ground shuddered as the shack was rocked to its foundations. I lost my footing, sliding across the floor, and Walter barely managed to pull me and Thomas out of the door before one of the walls collapsed.

All around us children were running from their own falling shelters.

But in eastern Coldharbour they were running for their lives.

Carnac.

I sensed him rise out of the ground – a massive eruption of soil and stone – and the first part of him that we saw was a clench-limb.

The clench-limbs of the newborn had been mere swellings. The one Carnac showed us was fully formed and fully extended and still warm from the heat of the earth. As soon as it was on the surface he flailed it across the ground, aiming to crush as many children as possible. If eastern Coldharbour hadn't been largely empty, thousands would have been killed in those first few seconds.

Then Carnac's head emerged. It was angular, with three black faceted eyes. His body, about twice the size of the newborn, followed it out of the gaping hole. His hair was slick and heavy like the Roar's. His teeth were arrayed in ranks.

And, after Carnac, came the Roar.

Her slashed abdomen thrust through the clouds and two clench-limbs plunged down. Their target was Milo. They reached not for his neck this time, but the huge cord-like bones supporting his wings.

Wanting to say something to steady everyone, Milo lowered his face between his shoulder-blades. Then he gave that up as impossible and simply flew.

'Come to me!' Walter bellowed, and the five of us scrambled onto his back. Shoving Jenny in the pouch, Walter tried to decide whether the main danger came from the Roar or Carnac. He made for the deepest of his underground tunnels, then realized it wouldn't be deep enough.

'Towards the beach!' I yelled. 'Head for the sea, Walter! I don't know what the Roar is going to do, but Carnac's after *us*. Get as far from him as you can!'

Jenny's birds went up. I couldn't believe the way they did that, flew up without hesitation to meet the danger. But the Roar was too huge for any number of birds to make a difference, and she ignored them, focusing entirely on Milo. Her clench-limbs were so powerful that his only chance lay in avoiding them. He did that, veering sideways, soaring up into the heavier clouds, then higher still, anything to keep his wings out of her reach.

I closed my eyes, seeking out the Roar's thoughts. If she

was fully occupied with Milo, she might accidentally reveal something.

No. She did not.

Walter ran southwards, towards the shore, and I looked back.

I shouldn't have. I should never have looked back to see Carnac, but I couldn't help it.

A child-family was running just ahead of his mouth.

Inside that mouth there were dark patches – tiny shapes swinging from the jaw and even inside his gums. For an appalling moment I thought Carnac was consuming children. Then I realized ordinary children could never have clung on the way these were doing.

The Unearthers. Dozens were embedded in Carnac. As I watched, he wrenched his whole head up in fury at their drills and flicked a clench-limb across his face. Several pairs were dislodged, falling the long distance to the ground; others hung on. But whatever the Unearthers did, I knew they were only an irritant; they could only delay Carnac.

He twisted his three eyes upward, towards his mother.

An instruction passed between them – her confirming how to find us – and Carnac swivelled in our direction.

He shook off a few more Unearthers – then heaved himself across the ground towards us.

Three things in that moment alerted me to the presence of the Protector. One was extra silver in the sky; another, a shout from Jenny; finally it was the twins, gazing open-mouthed towards the ocean. Dappled sunlight swept through me, and as I turned to follow it I witnessed the vast extents of the Evissas moving like a continent across Coldharbour.

Not dead, I realized. Not quite.

A series of piercing warning screams came from the Roar

– and Carnac pivoted to face the Protector – but he was too late. The Unearthers had distracted him for just long enough. Carnac managed to use a clench-limb to parry the first set of Evissas coming low over the ocean, but not the second. The Evissas swept in from the north, and there was no subtlety about their approach this time, no dexterous shaping of the digits. Fused into a solid mass three times Carnac's size, they hammered him into the earth.

The blow was so tremendous that everyone in Coldharbour except Walter was thrown to the ground.

I jumped up and glanced eastward again. Most of the Unearthers were lying motionless or barely moving in the mud, but some still clung tenaciously to Carnac. Half-crushed, he tried to fight on against the Protector. Then he seemed to realize that he could not, and retreated, dragging his damaged body back towards the gaping hole.

The Evissas hovered over him. There was plenty of time for the Protector to bring them down again, to finish Carnac off. Instead, in an almost tender gesture, he helped nudge Carnac back towards the hole.

It was only when I saw how slowly the Protector withdrew the Evissas back to the ocean that I realized how much effort it had cost him to take on Carnac this way. The Evissas barely made it back to the sea. They fell slackly under, and I felt only weariness.

'Rest,' I whispered. 'Will you rest?' It had taken everything the Protector had to react to Carnac. He had to rest now, but I knew he would not. Already his Evissas were straining upward again.

A flash of silver above, and our eyes turned to Milo. Somehow, while Carnac was the focus of the battle, he had managed to evade the Roar's clench-limbs, but he was tiring.

The Protector tried to help him. One set of Evissas feebly

resisted the drag of the waves, then fell again.

'Milo!' his voice boomed out desperately. 'I cannot reach you. I cannot!'

'No!' I shouted, realizing what the Protector was going to do next.

The ocean waters bulged, sections of the Protector's body emerging from the sea.

'What is it?' Emily pleaded, clutching at me.

'No! Don't!' I shouted, staring at the waves. 'Don't!'

'What's the matter?' Freda demanded. 'What is it? Helen, tell uz!'

'He can't,' I said, stammering out the words. 'He can't ... reach Milo ... so ... he's offering himself ... revealing his most vulnerable areas to the Roar. To distract her. To give Milo a chance.'

The Protector rose out of the water. He rose up, and it was like the slow lifting up of mountains. And as he did, I knew we had never truly seen silver before. Even on the darkest of nights, Milo had never shone like this. The whole sea was alight with it. The Protector arose, and we saw the underside of his head, and the upward tilt of his chest. We saw the arch of his throat and the vast tendons of his loins. Floods formed inside the ramparts of his back. Fissures radiated along his flanks, cracking and splitting open in ways that had no human meaning. And as he ascended I knew the Protector was emerging not just from our sea, but seas across the breadth of the world, skies everywhere brightening to his light.

His body lay prostrate across the ocean. For a moment it simply lay there, a pool of huge silver light.

Then came the response.

The Roar stopped attacking Milo. Briefly she hesitated – as if she could not believe her good fortune, or distrusted it

– then all four of her usable clench-limbs reached down the sky. The Protector's body lay horribly exposed, but he made no attempt to defend himself. He let the clench-limbs come. They felt their way across his body, spreading widely across the shining flesh as if choosing the place to strike out.

And while the clench-limbs were lowered, Milo acted. He folded his great wings. He brought them down and across the sky, a controlled sweep, each sharp wing-edge perfectly weighted, perfectly balanced. And as the wings came together, all but one of the Roar's clench-limbs was severed.

There was a scream of piteous loudness from above.

Then the Roar hurriedly withdrew her last clench-limb.

Two of the severed limbs fell into the sea. The third dropped over Coldharbour and would have crushed us, except that the Protector raised his Evissas and caught it.

The Roar was no longer visible. Where was she? Milo turned and turned in the sky, looking for her. I thought she must be gone. I couldn't believe she would attack again, after such a terrible loss, but I was wrong.

The clouds stirred afresh – and the Roar lowered her abdomen once more. Not much. A calculated amount. Just sufficient to present a target. In her eagerness, for a fraction of a second she let down her guard, and I knew what she intended to do.

'Stay away! Stay back!' I warned Milo.

Too far away, of course, for him to hear.

The Roar's abdomen was invitingly close. That's what it was – a tempter – and Milo reached for it. To do so he had to make an awkward turn, and the Roar knew that. As he manoeuvred, she thrust out her remaining clench-limb. The last of the Roar's clench-limbs finally caught Milo. It latched onto one of his wings. Latched onto the tip.

Latched on, held it – and snapped it off.

Milo suppressed a groan and beat both wings violently to keep himself aloft, but the Roar was not about to let him get away. She deployed a different weapon. A tooth came directly out of the sky, a great tooth, lowered on a great mouth. It slashed straight through Milo's east-facing wing, straight through it and into the ground below.

There were screams as everyone saw the hole torn through the wing, pinning Milo to the soil. Milo flailed uselessly for a few seconds in the mud, then realized that the only way he could break away from the tooth was to tear the wing loose. He did so, a terrible moment, then struggled aloft again, one of his wings beating powerfully, the other flapping like an immense ripped sheet in the wind.

Only willpower enabled him to sway back into the sky. We watched him swerve and nearly fall, then lift himself again, and while he did so his silver eyes never left the Roar. He stared at her. He fixed his sight on her as if his gaze alone could hold her at bay.

But then I sensed something new from the Roar.

I sensed her – relax.

It was intensely frightening. It was more frightening than anything that had come before. She relaxed. She stayed back – and simply watched Milo struggle. She must have known that with only one good wing he could no longer properly defend us. She hung back, and rather than risk getting any nearer simply loosed her poisons on him.

I didn't think the Roar had any poisons left, but she had, and now she let them rain down on Coldharbour at will.

This time there was no chance for Jenny's birds to respond.

Milo could have avoided the poisons. His manoeuvrability was still good enough for him to have managed that. He could have flown to safety. He could have flapped away over the ocean, escaped. Instead, he stretched his wings wide and tried to cover us.

And the poisons fell on him.

Only a moderate amount had fallen before. The amount falling from the Roar's abdomen now was unbelievable – a soft deadly blue rain across Coldharbour. Milo spread his wings to take it all. The poisons fell through the hole in his damaged wing, and to compensate he positioned his legs under it, and at first I thought he might contain all the poison. But it fell upon his chest, and upon his head, and ran around his eyes, and continued to rain on him and rain on him until finally even Milo's broad wings could take no more. They filled up with blue, until he could barely move them, they were so heavy with it.

And finally, when the wings were saturated, and the poison was seeping from the rest of his body across Coldharbour and falling on the children, he had no choice. For the first time since he had appeared over Coldharbour, Milo left his place over us and made for the ocean.

The Roar's weapons followed him. A few of those stabbing barbs I'd seen once before pursued him over the sea. They pursued him, but not for long. The Roar knew that Milo was finished. She did not want to take any more risks.

He did not get far. For a moment Milo hovered over the ocean, barely keeping himself there, and tried to say something to us. But he could not, and then he fell, not with grace, but with wings hard against his body, like a dead bird shot from the sky, and the first part of him that hit the ocean was his face. A huge spouting plume of water exploded as he hit the sea, and then another as his shoulders struck the waves. But it was his wings that made you weep, because even now they were so sleek that they slipped almost quietly into those waters.

Overhead, an eye of the Roar cut through the clouds. It cut through to watch Milo's body slowly sink, and I hated it, that eye, watching so closely, making sure.

And then it was over. Milo was no longer visible. There was no glimmer of him on the ocean surface, only the blue of the poisons spreading out, and the sight of grey whales, wanting to help Milo but unable to, having to flee the area, flee from his beautiful lost body.

We waited. We waited for any sign of him. Everyone stared in disbelief out to sea, unable to accept what had happened. We were all crying. Emily asked me if Milo was dead, but I must have given her a terrifying look because she didn't ask again.

Coldharbour lay in ruins. Tents and shacks were wrecked, members of the child-families scattered everywhere. Some of those who'd been in central Coldharbour when Milo's wing hit the ground had been crushed to death. In eastern Coldharbour many Unearthers were also dead, but I wasn't ready to think about that yet.

Youngsters across Coldharbour headed shakily towards the Barrier, in the hope of seeing a parent or relative. Others wanted to leave Coldharbour altogether, get in a boat and search the area where Milo had vanished. And everywhere you looked children were shielding their eyes. No wings to cover us from the sun now. The sight of it shining brightly overhead in the Milo-less sky was deeply disturbing.

We helped the injured as best we could. We buried the dead. Later I squatted outside the half-demolished shack, with Jenny staring at me accusingly with those dilated eyes I could do nothing for. The afternoon passed in a grey blur, and when evening came I was sure the night to follow would be our last. And then –

'What's wrong?' Thomas asked, seeing me wince.

I didn't answer.

'It's Carnac, isn't it?'

'Yes,' I said. 'He's dead. He just died from his injuries.'

I suppose that should have made us feel better, but it didn't. We'd had enough killing for one day. In any case, Carnac's death would probably only bring the Roar onto us sooner.

I kept one thing from the others – what was happening to Milo.

He was still alive, and I wanted to shout that out loud to everyone, but I didn't know if he would be by morning. The Protector was trying to save him. Deep under the waves their faces were linked, the Protector breathing for Milo, giving him air while also keeping him out of sight of the Roar.

It was Milo's reaction, though, that made me cry. He was concerned that the Protector's last dregs of energy would be used up in keeping him alive, and he didn't want that. So, under the sea, where no one could see the ripples, Milo flinched like a wounded bird against the Protector's face, attempting to slip quietly into the ocean.

It was the dark hours after midnight when the Protector finally contacted me. Dappled sunlight without words. Strength enough only for his thoughts now.

'It's my fault!' I cried out. 'I can't find the Roar's weakness. Tell me what to do! Please! I've tried everything!'

'Do not blame yourself,' the Protector murmured, 'or be so humble about your achievements. You have already looked into the abyss of the Roar's mind, and survived. Few have done that.'

A deep sadness then, almost the end of hope for himself. 'The final attack will be soon, Helen. The Roar will come for me while I am close to death and Milo lies injured and unable to intervene. It is the way of her kind. She is an assassin amongst assassins, this Roar; I might have prevailed if I had not come against this particular enemy. As for Milo, I will shield him for as long as I can, take what blows may be meant for him, but –'

'Don't die,' I said.

I said it out loud. I couldn't stop myself. I couldn't bear the idea of his thoughts not being in mine. I couldn't live without them now.

'You can,' the Protector replied at last. 'You can. Let me go, Helen. It has been my privilege to be present at the awakening of your species. A Protector is not always honoured by the acts of those it cares for, but your world has honoured me. Do you think a Protector ever did more than Milo to defend a world? *I* have been humbled by that. And when Thomas withheld his beauty from the Unearthers, would a Protector have held on for longer? No. Nor has a Protector given more than Walter, nor any shown more bravery than you did, Helen, when you walked back towards a child who had made you burn.

'I will take those memories when I leave,' he murmured. 'And others. Emily drowning, yet still struggling down to me. I'll take that with me as well. But it is not the end for you. Why should the Roar prevail? Your species felt her threat, and evolved to meet it. There is a transforming capacity to you all that is remarkable. The Roar fears you. She senses, as I do, that if you glimpse what you are capable of nothing will be the same.' He paused again. 'Promise me something. Promise me, Helen, that when I am dying you will leave me. Use the time I give you to find a way to defeat the Roar. Do you understand?'

'Yes,' I said automatically, just wanting to agree with him.

'No, Helen, I do not think so. Do you understand?'

I sat in the mud, crying.

'Don't die,' I whispered over and over, like a little girl. 'Don't.'

'I will not be unaccompanied when it happens,' he said softly. 'For will I not have your thoughts in mine? Thanks to you, I will not go alone into that dark place.' Then he said to me, 'The Roar is more frightened than you realize. Do what you can and I will be with you. Until the end of all things, I will guard you.'

I clung onto a last lingering dapple, then the Protector was gone.

Afterwards, seeing me lying there in the mud, Walter carried me across to the others. For a long time I just sat with Emily and Freda, staring numbly out across the sea and at the stars, trying not to think about the Protector.

I thought the night would end like that, surrounded by exhausted children, with the only question left being when the Roar would launch her final attack, but I was wrong. Towards the middle of the night something wonderful happened.

The light of stars was still pinpointing the sky when a boy sitting near our ruined shack shouted, 'Hey!' and jumped to his feet.

There was a silver gleam out over the sea. At first I thought it was the eye of the Protector. But it was not that. It was Milo. It looked as if the water had just borne him up, a lifeless thing on the waves. But then his face twitched and he weakly thrashed a wing, and as I wondered what was keeping his massive body from sinking, I saw what it was.

From some huge effort, the Protector, carrying Milo's weight to the surface, had brought him back to us.

Milo gasped as he drew in lungfuls of cool clean air. He

flexed his good wing. Then he arched his neck towards the sky, as if he must find a way to be there again. Moonlight slanted over his throat and he tried to lift his whole body up using his unbroken wing. The Protector said something soothing to him then that none of us could clearly hear, and laid his Evissas under Milo, held his face up, to give him air, to let him breathe.

If I could have ripped open my chest and given all the beauty to Milo in that moment, I would have. If a child had needed to kill me to take it, I'd have allowed them.

What was my beauty for, if not this?

Helen went back inside the shack – back to her lonely private battle against the Roar – and all we could do was wait. Every hour she failed to discover a weakness, Jenny grew more agitated. Eventually she left the pouch to be closer to me. Her eyes were fully dilated. She lifted her fringe to show me that she was ready.

The night passed, then morning, and throughout it Emily never took her eyes off the ocean. The Protector lay out there, trembling under Milo's weight.

'Those we love,' Emily whispered. 'Those we miss.'

'Those we love,' Freda said. 'Those we've kissed.' She took my arm, and asked, 'Is this the end of all things, Toms?'

And I thought – it may be.

Walter studied the skies. Keeping us all within arm's length he remained unnaturally still, surveying Coldharbour like some ancient god awaiting the end of the world.

From the shack, occasionally, I heard a scream of anguish from Helen.

And then another voice murmured in my ear. It wasn't one I'd ever expected to hear again.

'If I was the Roar,' it said, 'I'd attack now. What's she waiting for? Why doesn't she just finish this off and kill us all?' The coolness of steel settled on my shoulder 'Thought I was dead, eh?' Tanni said, managing a ghost of a smile. 'Well, that's no surprise.'

Parminder was still attached to him. One of her drills was partially broken. Looking more closely, I saw that Tanni was holding her up. Only thirty or so pairs of Unearthers were with them, and none of the younger ones.

'Sharper drills,' Tanni murmured, seeing my questioning glance. 'It meant the youngsters could get more easily under Carnac's skin. The rest of us fell off when he emerged. It saved our lives. We fell off. *I* fell off.' He swallowed. 'I didn't think the little kids would be much use, Thomas. Not really. Not when Carnac came up. I expected them to panic, but most didn't. They were smaller, lighter ... better than the older kids at slicing into him. None survived. Can you believe that? Not one. I made a promise, but I couldn't bring a single one out alive.'

He dropped his head, but I lifted it again and together we stared out at the two silver bodies across the sea.

At some point Emily put her hand on my neck. As she traced a line down my spine to the small of my back, I turned towards her, but she wasn't looking at me. She was looking at Walter.

And suddenly we were all looking at him, because he was sitting up and checking how close we were. Walter had always been the first of us to sense when the Roar was about to attack, and this time was no different. Almost calmly, without any emphasis, he announced, 'She's here.'

I'd waited all day for this moment. In my own way I'd even tried to prepare for the Roar's arrival, but I wasn't prepared. And perhaps I could never have been ready for what the Roar showed us, for this time it wasn't just her abdomen poking through the clouds. This time the Roar dipped herself more generously into Coldharbour's skies, and for the first time we saw her head.

The majority of children screamed when they saw it, and some ran, but not many. They wanted to but nearly all the shelters were wrecked. There was nowhere to run to.

Tanni barked a command, and the surviving Unearthers surrounded us – a thin ring of steel pointing at the head of the Roar.

That extraordinary head. We only saw part of it, because it was too big to fit across a single sky. And as it spread like a dark storm across the horizon, I'm not sure what aspects of it dismayed me most. Initially it was the jaw, the sheer length of time it took for the whole triangular black jut of it to descend. Then I noticed what was inside the jaw, and the ease with which the low-slung mouth slid outward to give the teeth free rein.

And, of course, the Roar had prepared a surprise for us as well: new objects, huge blade-like parts.

We should have known we hadn't yet seen all of her weapons.

Noticing Helen shudder, I knew the Roar had kept these new ones secret even from her. Neither Carnac nor the newborn had been equipped with these particular horrors. They hung like a forest from the Roar's face, a forest of blades. And, below those blades, swinging freely, was another weapon, one we knew only too well: a clench-limb – the last, still formidable clench-limb.

The Roar's head was directly over us. It was obvious that her target was no longer the Protector or Milo.

'It's me,' Helen said.

Nineteen

the blossoming mist

HELEN

Walter glanced agonizingly at the sky, preparing an escape –
but to where?

The clench-limb drifted over my head and, as it did so,
from the last reserves of his strength the Protector rose up
out of the ocean. Placing Milo in one of the long crevasses
of his back to keep him as safe as he could, he spread his
Evissas as a shield over Coldharbour.

Seeing that, the Roar ignored me and lowered herself
again over the sea. The side of her head creased open and a
slit appeared. From the slit five daggers of bone erupted
from her face on complex swinging joints.

A dense green mist immediately blossomed from the
Protector's limbs, partially hiding the Evissas.

The way the Roar responded made me realize that she
must have seen the mist before. Because she simply waited.
She did nothing. She waited. In the void of space the mist

might have been effective for longer, but Coldharbour's winds soon dispersed it.

Afterwards, for a moment, nothing happened. The two old adversaries simply stared at one another, as if dwelling on all the ages of battle there had ever been between them.

And then the Roar, keeping the daggers of bone in reserve, unleashed the bladed forest.

The blades detached themselves from the Roar's head and came in at several angles, choosing their own targets. Most went into the Protector, but a few went into Milo. The Protector frantically re-arranged Milo so that he would take less of the assault. Then he countered the bladed attack with both sets of Evissas. They flailed at the underside of the Roar's head, destroying some of the blades, but not all.

It was a brutal and slowly delivered battle. The bodies of the Roar and the Protector moved steadily, not quickly, over the water. For a long time the Evissas probed a bulging area on the Roar's neck. The Roar endured that and continued to use the bladed forest to devastating effect, taking huge pieces out of the flanks of the Protector – a precise exchange of close-quarter weaponry and power.

I looked again for a way to discover the Roar's weakness.

I couldn't find it. Of course not. I'd never succeeded in finding her frailties, even when I was new to her. How would I manage it now, when she was so much more on her guard?

Dad, I thought – and the moment I did, the Roar, as if teasing me, stretched her clench-limb towards his location outside northern Coldharbour.

Briefly she hesitated, and I sensed she was deciding whether to kill me and Dad immediately or finish off the Protector first. In the end, the decision was easily made. She had waited a long time to complete this particular kill, after all.

She chose the Protector.

into the ocean

THOMAS

Jenny writhed in Walter's arms, half out of her mind.

She needed my beauty – and how I wanted to give it! My face was hot. Her face was hot. Her dilated eyes invited me in. The twins tried to calm her, but there was no calming her. So much beauty was inside us and between us that we trembled with it.

But the clarity Jenny needed was still missing. Only one person could provide that. I glanced forlornly at Helen, and she shook her head, her face clenched with effort. 'I still can't find anything, Thomas. I can't!'

The outskirts of Coldharbour were now completely deserted of children. Over the past hours all the child-families had made their way towards me. They formed a single enormous group. Some looked at me; the rest looked at the sky over the ocean.

There was no let-up in the battle between the Roar and

the Protector. I couldn't be sure, but as the hours passed I became increasingly convinced that the Roar was actually enjoying the battle. Only once did she swivel her eyes towards us, and even then I think she was merely curious to see what we looked like. Once in a while she sent one massive weapon or other in a blaze of speed over Coldharbour, but it soon became clear that she did so only to expose the Protector more, because every time he had to shield us with his Evissas they were appallingly exposed to attack, and the Roar took casual chunks out of them.

Throughout the day and into the evening the battle raged. Sometimes Milo desperately tried to take some of the blows meant for the Protector, but the Protector would not allow that.

By nightfall everyone knew that the Protector was losing the battle. During the day there had been intervals when he seemed to be holding his own, but no amount of wishful thinking could convince even the twins that was true any more. It was Walter who finally said what none of us had dared to say:

'The Protector's dying.'

And after that it became truly terrible to watch, because of course the end would not come quickly. We should have realized that nothing as large as the Protector could have died quickly, even if it had wanted to. As the Protector weakened the Roar gradually slowed down her attack: deliberately flourishing her weapons in a more leisurely way, clearly wanting to extend the pleasure she took from every blow.

All night the Protector's bright face was gradually dragged out of the sea towards the worst of the Roar's weaponry. He resisted, but the clench-limb would not let up, smashing over and over into the Protector's sensitive flanks, and though the Evissas struck back they were always blocked now, and eventually the Roar disregarded them altogether.

At some point Walter stood up. Sensing the battle was lost, he searched for a place to take us. But there was nowhere safe. How could there be? Even if Walter could have run from Coldharbour, there was no hiding from the Roar.

'We'll form a guard,' Tanni yelled, and the Unearthers swung in front and behind us.

'Jenny!' Walter ordered. 'The b-birds! Cover us. Screen us with the birds.'

She started to – but she couldn't concentrate for long enough. Anyway, I think she knew the birds would make no difference now.

'Help us, Helen,' she pleaded. 'Help us.'

I couldn't believe the Protector would continue to fight on, but he did. He did not give way, and throughout the night the onslaught continued and still he did not give way. And then, with dawn arriving, pink and strangely bright under the dark jaw of the Roar, the fight seemed to turn decisively. The Protector still thrust with his Evissas, but not tellingly, and the Roar dealt with them more and more easily until, late in the morning, she was able to drag the daggers of bone that had been waiting so long for him across the upper part of the Protector's neck. There followed a scream as half the digits on one of the Evissas, moving to guard that place, were ripped away. Afterwards the Protector hurriedly cloaked himself in more mist, but the Roar was no longer confused, and finally her clench-limb was utterly fixed to the face of the Protector and heaving it upward, upward out of the ocean.

The Protector could no longer hold it back. Barbs with spiked tips, dropping in accurate flurries, calmly ripped him to shreds.

And my heart sank when I saw what happened next, because I knew it was nearly the end. For when Milo again tried to slip away from the Protector, this time the Protector allowed him to. He let Milo fall, in his final desperation let Milo sink into the ocean.

Twenty one

a rich and terrifying beauty

HELEN

Wings folded against his back, Milo fell to the ocean bottom, and I followed him there, under the waves, into the blackness.

'No, Helen. Have you still not learned?'

The Protector. Finding a way to speak to me one last time.

He was about to die. I knew that because he did something he had never done before. He opened up the whole of his mind, to show me what I'd always wanted to see – the other Protectors.

I saw them. I saw the appalling choices they had been forced to make about which planets to defend. I saw the final choice they made for *our* Protector – sent too young to our world, knowing there was no choice. Nothing was withheld from me now.

'Look not upon my wounds, Helen,' the Protector said, 'but on what you can still do.'

'I've tried everything,' I whispered.

'Everything?'

'If the Roar was ever frightened of me, she isn't any more.'

'But there is one who is. She has never lost her fear.'

The second newborn, I thought. But she would never leave the Roar now.

'You think nothing would tempt her down?' the Protector thought. 'Denied any part in the battle, she aches for my flesh. It is only fear that holds her back from it. If she had no fear the newborn would feed on me. She would do it while I am still alive. That is the Roar way.'

I shuddered, knowing it was true.

The Protector's voice was virtually gone. 'Helen, what would give the newborn the courage to fly down to me?'

Only one thing, I thought. Only one thing would entice even this easily frightened newborn from her mother.

Death itself. The death of the Protector.

There was silence between us.

'To defy the Roar's weaponry a little longer serves no further purpose now,' the Protector murmured at last. 'Indeed, it only gives her satisfaction. In choosing the manner and moment of my own death I will at least cheat her of that. Wait for it, and you may yet discover what you need from the Roar.' When I started to object, the Protector hushed me. 'Death is only death, Helen. I am afraid, but I am ready for it. Are you?'

I couldn't answer that. Beside me, Thomas was kneeling next to Jenny, his whole face shaking with a rich and terrifying beauty he could not release.

Jenny gazed back at him. Her eyes were empty.

They were both ready.

If I'd had any doubt about that before, I had none now.

The newborn was like a little pearl of excitement as I

slipped into her mind. There she was, would-be murderer, hanging impatiently from the thickest hairs of her mother. With the battle almost won, she could not wait to take part in the final slaughter.

Tiny newborn, brought up to kill; how much she wanted her first kill now!

The Protector waited. He held on to his life, waiting for me to be ready.

And when I was, or as ready as I would ever be, I felt a wordless sigh as his body fell limp.

He collapsed, the whole weight of him, into the sea.

The Roar let him fall. Her thread-rapiers and barbs retracted, and she watched the Protector drop away from the daggers of bone and strike the ocean. A huge plume of water rose up and splashed over Coldharbour, and it was like being drenched with silver. Then the Protector's body sank, and though it sank quickly, there was so much of him that his departure was not swift.

His Evissas were the last part of him to leave us. I could barely recognize the shape of them any longer, they were so damaged, and as they slipped into the sea I wanted more than anything to follow the Protector's mind there, under the cold water.

I went, instead, to the newborn.

And she was frightened, our eager little newborn. Frightened not for herself, but of missing out on the kill. She wanted to savour the Protector's flesh. As the last of him faded beneath the waves, before it was too late she ripped the sheaths off her teeth. She opened out her jaw – and flew at him.

The Roar reacted immediately – sending her clench-limb down to fetch the newborn back. But it was not easy. The clench-limb was never meant for her own kind, and the newborn resisted her. The Roar could not find a hold.

For an instant the Roar's mind opened a crack to me.

'Thomas!' I shouted.

'It's yours,' he said.

I'd never been able to use his beauty before, but in that moment no one had a need greater than mine, and I took it. I seized it.

Too late, the Roar realized that I was inside her mind, penetrating her defences. She desperately raised more against me, but it made no difference; I tore those down as well.

I entered her depths. I entered the regions even her newborn had never been.

The strongest of living things is not all strength. The best-concealed weakness is still a weakness. The Roar had few weaknesses, but she could no longer hide them from me. Realizing that, she shrieked and shrieked to distract me. It made no difference.

I looked into the heart of her.

The newborn, hearing her mother, flew back, no longer thinking of the kill.

I glanced at Jenny, and she was already changing.

'What's happening?' Walter cried, as she toppled from his arms.

'The birth of a weapon,' I said.

Jenny's red dress disappeared. Her legs disappeared. Her arms withered. When that happened, children ran in fear and Walter and the Unearthers had to tighten the steel ring to stop them crushing us.

Jenny's hands were no longer her hands.

'Get away from me!' she screamed. 'Get away!'

And we did. Even Walter, hearing that scream, knew he had to.

Jenny's body rotated sideways. Her neck disappeared. Her

head disappeared. Then four large prongs emerged where her limbs had been. There was one more change: a subtler one, an extra flap of skin. It appeared behind her eyes.

'What's that f-for?' Walter gasped.

I didn't answer. I stayed focused, and the next thing I witnessed was not one I'd ever expected to see.

It was the Roar, terrified; the Roar, in horror, fleeing our skies.

For she knew; somehow she understood. She realized that whatever weapon Jenny had become, this time it was not an error or mistake. Flying upwards, the newborn clinging to her hairs, she desperately tried to escape.

Jenny hesitated a moment, altering her angle to match the Roar's.

Then she launched herself.

The speed with which she approached the Roar was incredible, and I think the Roar knew that her only chance was to stop Jenny before she reached her.

The clench-limb came down. It was still the best defence the Roar had, and she did not panic as she deployed it. She remained calm, ignored the mewling newborn, and sifted through all her experience as an assassin to find a manoeuvre that would block Jenny. Sweeping all three of her eyes to her underside, she plotted Jenny's trajectory. Then the clench-limb reached down. Its velocity hurtling across the sky was overwhelming. It matched Jenny's speed and arc of ascent, and for a second I thought Jenny would be swallowed inside its grasp, but at the last moment she evaded it.

Jenny was beyond the clench-limb.

The Roar changed tactics instantly, staying composed, improvising, dropping the thread-rapiers and bladed forest in Jenny's path. But Jenny was small enough to slip between them, and suddenly the Roar's daggers of bone, designed to impale the face of a Protector, looked clumsy.

In dismay, the Roar opened up the slits of her face for more weapons, but Jenny was already beyond them. She flew on, sliding deftly in and out of the Roar's thick body hair, moving downward.

The Roar did not know what part of her body Jenny would target. And then, as Jenny headed deep under her flanks, finally she did. In that moment, at last, I felt the Roar panic. She panicked and heaved her swollen abdomen despairingly up. But Jenny followed her, followed her beyond the clouds, and before the Roar could reach the sanctuary of space she attached herself to the tough skin of the abdomen.

The four prongs. The Roar at last understood their purpose. They had mystified her, but now she knew, and all her composure vanished.

Four prongs, each spiked with a roughened tip, each fashioned specifically to rupture the poison sacs of the Roar.

The Roar could do nothing to stop them.

They slashed through – and the sacs exploded like bursting rivers.

Poison erupted into the body of the Roar. Poison. So much poison. And it shouldn't have mattered – the Roar was immune to significant amounts of it – but the poison had proven such an effective weapon against us that she had created more than the usual amount in her deadly mixing chambers, and she could not take this much. Her body was not designed to absorb this amount, and as it entered her the Roar screamed. She screamed and writhed, twisting and churning with the effort to expel the toxins before they killed her.

Back she brought her clench-limb, tearing deep inside her own flesh this time to rip out the sacs, but it was too late, and then the Roar made another decision. When she realized the poisons would eventually kill her anyway, her clench-limb reached for something else.

For her newborn.

It was not the caress the newborn mistook it for. The grasp was meant to kill. The Roar would kill her own child rather than accept the shame of defeat.

No, I thought – and in response Jenny streamed ahead of the clench-limb. She dived under the Roar's coarse body hair, and removed a cube-shaped object.

The newborn – being separated from her mother.

The Roar shrieked over and over as she fought to get at her child, but already the newborn was too distant for even her sifts to reach out and strangle.

The Roar had one more weapon at her disposal. A final trick none of us had seen her use. She led Jenny beyond our world altogether, into deep space, and there followed a brilliant flash of light. It was so intense that even in Coldharbour everyone shielded their eyes against it.

Emily stared at me.

'A last attempt to stop Jenny,' I said, thinking of the second flap of skin. 'A light to burn out the retinas of her eyes. It hasn't worked.'

Twenty two

more than human

THOMAS

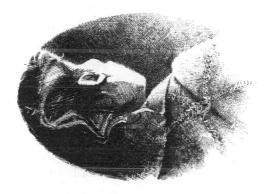

Silence across Coldharbour. For a long time there was just silence. At the Barrier it was the same, as the parents also tried to come to terms with what they had just seen. I lay in Walter's arms, exhausted. Helen crept across the mud to be with me. The twins, their skinny legs shaking, joined her, the four of us huddling under the protective arms of Walter.

And as we lay there, the world above Coldharbour was transformed.

First the blinding light faded, and then, surprising everyone, the sun reappeared in the sky, shining down on us again. It was an unnerving moment: warmth after the deep gloom of the Roar. I looked around, and the only reminders of her presence were tattered clouds whirring crazily in the sky and the ocean itself, still carrying traces of her poisons towards the shore. When the swells finally subsided they left a dazzlingly blue deposit on the beach sands.

Then, beyond the sands – a disturbance.

I knew who it must be, though I couldn't see him yet.

A region of silver spread under the ocean. It was followed by the beginnings of a huge face. The lower parts of his head were lifted by grey and hump-backed whales. And after the head came a wing, slapping the surface in a welter of blood.

'M-Milo,' Walter said.

He floated to the surface. For a moment he rested in the surf, supported by the whales, rested and caught his breath. Then he used his good wing to drag himself onto the deserted beaches. The poisons made him wince as he hauled his weight over them, but soon he was beyond the blue sands and scraping his way along the estuary. There he stopped. He coughed and the weight of streams burst from his lips. Turning his head on its side he faced us, illuminating Coldharbour. With every breath I felt the tides of air rush into his lungs. We watched him. We could not take our eyes off him. And in the end we had been watching for so long that a sunset spread like a gentle fire behind him in the west.

Evening in Coldharbour. A normal evening, except for strange contrary breezes as the weather settled down in the aftermath of the battle.

But how could we enjoy it? Once we knew Milo was safe, there was only one thought on everyone's minds.

'The Protector ain't dead, Toms!' Emily said fiercely. 'Not quite. Not yet. We'd know if ee was! C'mon, use yer beauty for 'im! C'mon …' She started dragging me towards the sea, but Helen shook her head.

'No amount of beauty can help him now,' she said. 'It's too late.'

I thought the twins were going to hit Helen then. Instead, Emily held out both her hands to Freda. 'Let's go down to 'im,' she whispered. 'Ee shouldn't be alone. Ee's lived so long, ee can't imagine what it's going to be like to die, not really. Let's be wiv 'im when it happens.'

Freda nodded, but before she could climb onto Walter's back, Helen stared thoughtfully at me.

'What about you, Thomas?' she said. 'Don't you want to visit the Protector before he dies?'

'But my beauty – '

'Can't carry you under the sea?' She arched her brows. 'I think it will now. In any case, you should try, because the Protector's asking for you.'

'For me?'

'For you, Thomas. He has something to tell you.'

I didn't know what Helen meant, but before I could ask the twins yanked my arm, anxious to be underway, Walter prodded me onto his shoulder, and we were off.

There was no conversation on the journey across Coldharbour. The twins were quiet, their freckled legs clinging to Walter's knees while I hung on grimly to his neck.

The ocean. Walter picked his way through the poisons lining the beaches, and suddenly we were in the water. Emily supported my neck, remembering what it had been like to drink in those waves for the first time. 'Trust yer beauty,' she whispered.

'It's OK, Toms,' Emily said, taking my arm. 'We're here. We won't let anything hurt yer. How could we?'

The first few laps of water against my shins were unbelievably cold. Walter stood nearby, there if I needed him. I looked inside myself, and realized that Helen was right: my beauty wasn't only for others now; there was a little inside for me. I glanced at Walter once more, then lowered my head, parted my lips and let my beauty offer up a first taste of the sea.

We travelled into the depths, and as we did Freda put her hand over her heart. 'We're the lucky ones,' she mouthed. 'To be chosen like this. To be able to see 'im one last time.'

Colder and darker it became, until it was no longer quite so cold or dark. And then I saw the crevices decorating his back – the long spread of him on the tides of the deep.

The twins escorted me along the Protector's neck, to his face. They placed me there, in a fold near the hills of his lips. I had many questions, but for some reason now that I was here I didn't feel the need to ask anything. Though there wasn't much time left, the Protector let us rest. The twins luxuriated in the warm feel of his skin. Pressing their shoulders up against him, they listened to the lap of the ocean against his body. Taking my lead from them, I settled my head against his lips and lay there, gazing up. From down here our own ocean looked as if it belonged to another world.

I wondered about that. If my beauty could take Jenny into space, could it take us as far as other worlds?

'Do you really think that is all it can do?' said a voice.

The Protector. The vibration of his words through the water.

'What would you ask of your beauty,' he said gently, 'if you could ask for anything? If there was no possibility of failure, Thomas, what would you ask of it?'

I didn't understand, and I think he knew that.

'Your beauty could take you to another world,' the Protector said, 'but why limit yourself to such idle excursions? Everyone is waiting, Thomas. Waiting for you. Milo encouraged the children to Coldharbour, but it is your beauty that haunts them. Do you still need the Roar hovering overhead to be ready to use it?'

I swallowed, still unsure what he meant.

'Should we become ... more like you?' I asked. 'More like Protectors, so that we can fight the Roars?'

Laughter followed that, a slight rustle.

'You think these silver flanks are the limit of what you can be? Do you really think that is the limit to what your species can become? No. Your beauty is no longer the tame force it once was, Thomas. It is no longer tame at all.' He paused. Then he said:

'ARE YOU READY?'

His words passed through me like a wind. It was the same wind I'd felt when Milo had asked the same question all those weeks ago. And I wanted to say yes. I wanted more than anything to say yes, but I wasn't even sure what the Protector meant.

He said nothing more to me, but they were not the Protector's last words. He saved those for the twins. It was time for them to take their leave of him, and I didn't watch that moment, or listen in. It belonged to them.

Afterwards, Emily's tears mixed with the ocean as she fumbled for one of my hands, Freda found the other, and together we swam up. The water was silver, then less so, then grey, and finally black as we left the last of the Protector behind.

On the way I searched my heart, or tried to anyway. I questioned my beauty. It wasn't quite the same, I knew that. Was a new kind of blood brimming there? Perhaps. Whatever it was moved faster than before, and, thinking of the Protector's words, I was afraid of it.

Late evening in Coldharbour, and Walter had barely carried us back to the shack when Helen whispered, 'Parents.'

The Barrier had been down for hours, but the sheer

numbers of people meant it had taken them all this time to make their way safely inside Coldharbour. It was around dawn before they reached our area, and the first parents to find us were Tanni's. It was an awkward meeting. They weren't quite sure what to make of their drill-handed son – or his firm attachment to this odd dark-haired girl – but Tanni shrugged that off.

'This is Parminder,' he said, standing up. 'She tells jokes. Some of them' – he smiled – 'are rubbish. And this is ...' It took a long time to complete the introductions, because Tanni made a point of naming every single surviving Unearther. Afterwards, he named all the dead ones, too. And while he insisted on that, and starting up a search for their parents, midday arrived, and I suppose we should have eaten, but so much was happening that nobody thought of it.

It was an extraordinary afternoon in every way. The air was full of tears and laughter as children and parents across Coldharbour gradually found each other. Helen helped Walter locate his own parents, and the three of them made their way for a time towards Milo. Then the twins' mum – there was no mistaking that vibrant red hair – staggered forward, and Emily and Freda jumped on her and dragged her into the semi-privacy of Walter's half-demolished hut.

Helen remained with me outside the shack. At some point she lifted my right hand. Her hair fell ticklishly over my wrist.

'Look,' she said, pointing at the sky.

It was the birds – leaving Coldharbour at last. We watched them go. Milo also managed to raise his head in recognition of what they had done, and each flock wheeled over him three times before departing.

The whales were amongst the last animals to leave. They

gathered in their family shoals, then started the long journey home. Those from the southern part of our world had no homes left to go to, but part of me sensed that by the time they arrived we could change that if we wished.

Evening settled in; a peaceful, warm evening with barely a trace of wind, and suddenly Helen's face lit up.

'It's y-your dad, isn't it?' I said.

She nodded.

I looked around. 'I can't s-see him.'

'Neither can I yet,' she replied, laughing. It didn't matter, of course – you only had to take one look at her face to see that she was with him anyway. But the rest of us didn't want to wait for him, so Helen gave directions and finally Walter braved the crowds and brought him back to us on those wide and comfortable shoulders of his.

Afterwards, Walter collected us all together: his own parents, me, Helen and her dad, the twins and their red-haired mum, Tanni and Parminder. Then the twins reached out for some food they'd been keeping somewhere out of sight and Walter helped them set out a make-shift meal. Following that, he insisted that we get some sleep. I explained to him that there was no way I'd sleep, but he pressed my head none too delicately against a mattress, and before I knew it my eyes were shut.

When I awoke the stars were out and Walter was still beside me. I think he'd been lying next to me all night, and looking at him I realized that I was seeing something strange. Closed eyes. His eyes were closed. Walter was sleeping. I'd never seen him do that before, and tried to sneak out of bed to avoid waking him, but as soon as I stirred he was up as well, insisting on staying near me.

We stood outside for a while, watching parents *still*

tramping into Coldharbour.

In the morning the hazel-eyed girl came to say goodbye. She touched my hand, laughing at the memory, and departed with a huge child-family, with no need for a final backward glance.

After another improvised meal, Walter scooped us up again and jogged southwards along the river estuary to be with Milo.

Milo: that remarkable face! I liked being close to it – the way it towered over us – and I was also aware of something else: my beauty entering him. It had been happening for hours; there was no mistaking the tell-tale way he drew it from me.

For a while we all just stayed together in the shadow of Milo's brightness, talking quietly, filthy because we'd been sitting for hours in the mud, but not caring about it. Except for the twins, that is – who surreptitiously slipped away to wash and change. 'Priorities,' Emily told me, and Walter grinned away.

Seeing that, Emily climbed up his jacket and tapped his teeth.

'If I'd that smile, I'd open wide,' she said.

'If I'd that smile, I wouldn't hide,' Freda said.

The morning passed slowly, and then my beauty gave me a signal.

Youngsters all around started shouting with excitement.

I stood up and everyone stood with me.

Hesitantly at first, waiting for us and other children to back off, then more assuredly, Milo spread his wings. The broken one was repaired enough to be used now, and he was anxious to be aloft again.

He rose into the sky, and I expected him to take his old place over us, but he didn't.

'DO NOT BE AFRAID,' he called down, seeing everyone staring nervously up at him. 'THE ROAR HAS GONE, AND THE REST OF HER KIND, WHEN THEY FIND US, WILL NOT FIND US THE SAME. I AM LEAVING, BUT I WILL NOT BE LONG. THERE ARE MORE TO DISCOVER AND MORE TO BRING.'

And with that he soared away from Coldharbour, until he was a distant silver speck on the southern horizon.

'He's going for the others,' Helen said.

'The others?' I asked.

'The rest of the children. The ones who never made it to Coldharbour. He's gone to collect them.'

I shaded my eyes, but already Milo was too far away to see. The last of his silver lingered in the skies overhead, then faded altogether. I looked at those skies. I looked hard. Without Milo or the Protector to light them we were no longer a silver world. The sky was blue, the sun yellow, the clouds shades of dark and light. I had no idea if they would stay that way, or if we might need to change them, or even if it mattered.

I thought about Milo, what he'd done for us.

'Even so, he's ready for a greater challenge,' Helen said.

I peered up, and as I did so I could see birds, birds everywhere. The flocks were returning. They flew around our heads, having changed their minds about going home.

'All over the world it's happening,' Helen said. 'The animals are ready for another challenge as well. They don't just want to go home.'

'But Jenny hasn't even come back yet.'

'She won't be long.'

'What's she going to do with them all?'

'Jenny doesn't know yet. But she will.' Helen gazed at me. 'Are you ready, Thomas?'

My throat felt dry.

'Don't you realize yet?' she said. 'Don't you understand what your beauty can do?'

Before I could think about that, Jenny returned to us.

The four prongs were gone and the extra flap of skin over the eye. There were no more signs of the weapon. By the time she alighted in the soil next to us she was just a little girl again, surrounded by birds, holding out her arms impatiently for Walter.

Everyone, of course, wanted to know what had happened to the Roar.

'Jenny's shackled her on the moon,' Helen said. 'Separated her from the newborn and imprisoned them both there. The newborn is safe, but beyond her reach. The Roar will live for some time yet. I'm not sure what to do about the newborn.'

Parminder, standing nearby, said, 'Shouldn't we kill them? We should kill them, Helen. Kill them both.'

'Perhaps.'

'What do you mean – '

'Listen,' Helen whispered.

I couldn't hear anything at first. Then a noise carried to us.

The Roar. There was no doubting it. It was one of her screams. But not like the ones we had heard before. This scream was higher pitched and continuous.

'A call,' Helen said. 'The final humiliation of the assassin – a call for help. Before she dies, she's bringing the others towards us, the rest of the Roars.'

'What?' I stared at her in disbelief. 'What's the matter with you? Stop her before they hear it!'

'Should we?'

'Yes!' I turned for support to Walter, but found none.

'Sooner or l-later we have to face them,' he said.

'Why should they choose the time and place?' Helen added. 'Let them come to us.'

'But how many are there?'

'Thousands just in our part of the galaxy,' she said. 'And the nearest assassin-team is closer than the Protector realized.'

'How can you know that? I thought you couldn't detect minds so far away.'

She gave me a mysterious look, completely unlike her. 'I couldn't. That's changed now.'

I sat there, imagining the dark hulking bodies of the Roars turning in space, heading for us. Thousands. I couldn't imagine thousands. I couldn't imagine any amount of beauty able to deal with so many.

Helen said, 'They're killing the Protectors, Thomas. Every moment we leave the Roars out there, the few remaining Protectors are being picked off by the assassin-teams, one by one.'

I felt my beauty flutter, making calculations I could not even begin to comprehend.

I turned to the twins. Sitting nearby, either side of their mum, their nails scraped the dry soil, the hems of their dresses held miraculously just above the muck. They were the same girls I'd always known, their skinny legs so natural to me now that I couldn't imagine them any other way. They showed no immediate desire for my beauty to turn them into anything else, and I was grateful for that. Even if my beauty was capable of it, I wasn't ready to see all children change yet.

'Is that all you're worried about?' Helen said, putting her hand against my cheek. 'Your beauty will not change *who* they are. It won't change that. But our bodies have to be able to confront the Roars in space. And we should go now. If we wait, the Roars will kill more of the Protectors on their journey towards us.'

'I don't understand what you're asking,' I said, suddenly feeling angry with her. 'You're expecting too much.'

'Am I, Thomas? The Protectors can't look after us any more. They can't even look after themselves. There are too few of them.' She stared at me. 'Milo wasn't silver by accident. He was silver because he sensed the role we would have. Don't you understand yet? Don't you see? There's no one left to protect the other worlds from the Roars.'

'Meaning what?'

'Meaning it's up to us now.'

'Us?'

'Thomas, *we* have to become the new Protectors.'

I couldn't take that in.

'I ... my beauty can't do that,' I said. 'I ... haven't got enough to turn us into that.'

'Haven't you?'

I swallowed thickly. I looked at Helen, and as I did I felt afraid because I knew something. I suddenly knew there was no mind she could not read, no threat she could not anticipate. I turned to Jenny, tucked into Walter's side, and realized that there was no weapon she would not be able to equal.

There were millions of children around us. Only a fraction of those inside Coldharbour had been changed so far by my beauty. It hadn't touched them in any way, not yet. But it could. I didn't have to look at them to realize that they were ready for it. I only had to examine my beauty to know that.

I let it loose, carefully – only a light beauty-touch, just enough to reach the nearest children – and as I did so I seemed to see something. It was the opening of a doorway. I'd seen that doorway once before. It was a doorway into summer, the same one Helen and I had glimpsed when those first gang kids came breathlessly running across Coldharbour all those weeks ago. I'd told Helen I was ready then, but I hadn't been.

Walter came to stand beside me. Some of his visitors were still close by his side, but most had left to join child-families. As I gazed at them, I knew that they didn't need him any more. He'd taught them to be independent, to find someone else to help.

'Yes. They're ready for something greater, too,' Helen said, locking her eyes into me.

I glanced at Walter, and he smiled. It was me, I realized, who needed his support more than anyone else now. That's why he'd been edging closer to me all day.

'It's all r-right, Tommy,' he said, reading the fear on my face. 'I'm here.'

His hands closed around my head like a shield.

I parted his fingers, just as I'd seen Jenny do so often, and gazed out. Tanni lounged nearby, watching me. I studied his drills, knowing that I could get rid of them now.

'No,' he said, when I fingered them.

'Don't you want to be the way you were at least?'

'Maybe,' he said. 'But why settle for that? Don't you have a longing for something else, Thomas? Something more. Shouldn't we want to be more than human?'

The twins snuggled up against me. I glanced at them, then turned away to look at the sky. A few stray cumulous clouds were drifting across it, carried on a breeze that lifted white-caps off the sea. Each wave brought small slicks of iridescent blue poison onto Coldharbour's beaches. I left them that way for now, knowing that we could change them whenever we wished. Or, rather, that my beauty would give the children the power they needed to do so.

I gazed at them all. I gazed at Helen – and this time it was she who appeared momentarily afraid.

My beauty stirred, and every child in the world felt its motion.

The Protector, from the ocean depths, from his last breaths, felt its motion, and shuddered in awe. Helen was wrong. She didn't know the limits of my beauty, after all.

I knew there was still time to save the Protector.

The Roar shrieked and shrieked – and this time it was a different call – one to warn the Roars away.

Too late. No matter where they went, we would find them. I had no idea what we would do when we did.

I felt the summer pouring in.

Milo was overhead again, children on his wings, his eyes flashing in all directions.

'It's a long way to the most distant of the Roars,' Helen said.

Walter wiped her shoes and picked her out of the mud. He helped her dad climb onto his back, and the other parents. He eased Tanni and Parminder up onto his shoulders. He nudged Emily and Freda onto his knees. Jenny sniffed, wiped her hands on his trousers, and crept into the security of his pouch. When they were all in place, Walter turned to me.

'I'm ready,' I said.